Tea for two and a piece of cake

Tea for two and a piece of cake

PREETI SHENOY

RANDOM HOUSE INDIA

Published by Random House India in 2012
Sixth impression in 2014

Random House Publishers India Pvt. Ltd.
7th Floor, Infinity Tower C, DLF Cyber City,
Gurgaon – 122002, Haryana

Random House Group Limited
20 Vauxhall Bridge Road
London SW1V 2SA
United Kingdom

ISBN 978 81 8400 279 9

Typeset in Galliard BT by InoSoft Systems, Noida

Printed and bound in India by Replika Press Private Limited

For Satish,
who makes it all worthwhile with his
unwavering faith in me.
This one is for you, my love.

Our share of night to bear,
Our share of morning,
Our blank in bliss to fill,
Our blank in scorning.

Here a star, and there a star,
Some lose their way.
Here a mist, and there a mist,
Afterwards—day!

—Emily Dickinson (1830–86)

Contents

Prologue

I am bathing our seven-month-old baby boy when my husband calls to tell me that our marriage of eight years is over. I rush out of the bathroom, wrap the baby in a towel and am cradling the phone in my ear, with one hand on the baby to prevent him from rolling over the bed, and go crashing to the floor. My hands are still wet, and I wipe them hurriedly as I pick up the phone. When my husband tells me in a calm voice that it is over and he is leaving me, I fail to comprehend.

Then my heart starts beating at what feels like a thousand beats a minute. No, it starts pounding and all I can hear is his steely calm voice saying, 'Hello—you there?'

If this was a scene in a movie, this would probably be the moment when I drop the phone and collapse in shock on the bed while a melancholic soundtrack is introduced in the background. But this is real life and all I feel, at least right now, which is the beginning (but I am yet to know it), is that he is playing some sort of a cruel joke on me. But it isn't the first of April and it is the steeliness and edge in his voice that shakes me up.

I do not know what to say. So all I do is answer his question.

'Yes, I am here,' I hear myself say, my hand still on baby Rohit, who is gurgling in delight as he always does after a warm bath.

'I am sorry it has to come to this,' he says. But the steel in his voice does not go away. And he does not sound sorry at all. In fact, there is no trace of emotion in his voice.

'Look, Rohit needs his feed and nap. I have to go,' I say and hang up, choosing to ignore this sword that has been driven right into me. But there is a silent scream inside my head which I am unable to stop. It continues in the background like a supporting orchestra.

I carry Rohit to his high chair and strap him in. I prepare his baby food on auto mode. I even manage to sing his favourite rhyme and make him have his full quota of baby cereal. 'He would make a good model for an advert of baby food,' I think to myself. He is chubby and bubbly and the twinkle in his eyes refuses to dim, a lot like his dad.

I try to think of everything besides Samir's phone call to me. I cannot believe him having said something like this. Ours is a happy marriage. Or so I had thought. This has come as a total bolt from the blue. Or perhaps the signs were already there, but I had chosen to ignore them, subtly brushing them away under the bliss of domesticity, amidst Rohit's giggles and seven-year-old Tanya's endless chatter. I don't know.

But surely our marriage isn't so bad? Conversations like these happen only when there are years of hurt, years of pent-up frustration, and years of fighting. We haven't even been fighting of late. I don't even remember when we fought the last time. I have always been patient and, whatever be my weak points, one of the greatest strengths I pride myself on is never losing my temper.

I am lying next to Rohit, patting him absent-mindedly. He is a good baby and drops off to sleep within minutes. Thoughts are whirling around in my head. I realize I am involuntarily holding my breath. I exhale slowly with a deep, long sigh. What have I been missing? Why is this happening to me? How can he say something like this? I have no clue. I have always tried hard to please him. I have kept our sprawling home immaculately clean. I have never complained about his late-night office parties. Above all, I have been a good wife and a great mother, even if I may say so myself. Yes, I admit I may have put on a bit of a weight since baby Rohit came, but surely nobody leaves a spouse for this reason?

I truly do not know what to do. Tanya's school bus will be arriving anytime now and once she comes, it will be a mad rigmarole of trying to divide my time between two children and trying to get dinner organized, issuing instructions to the cook and overseeing that the vegetables and rotis are made just the way Samir likes them. He is fussy about his food, but a sweet guy otherwise.

The kind of sweet guy who has just told his wife of eight years that their marriage is over.

And he has chosen to do it over the phone.

Is there another woman in his life? Does the cliché 'the wife is always the last to know' hold true after all? I have no idea.

All I know is Rohit and Tanya need me right now. So I forcefully shove aside the disturbing phone call and pick up Rohit who has now woken up from his nap. Holding him in my lap, I open the door to let Tanya in, greeting her chirpily as she enters.

I am frightened, upset, hurt. I am not yet shattered or devastated. That is to come later. Yet I am not angry. My world as I know it has just come crashing down, but I am still smiling, still pretending, and still being a perfect mummy, hugging Tanya, listening to her chatter, serving her a snack as though nothing is amiss.

Time has never crawled this slowly before. I keep glancing at the clock, waiting for him to come home to make sense of it all. I am so afraid to call him. I am terrified of what he is going to say. I have no guts to face him or this fireball that he has bombarded me with. I want to duck, but I am frozen.

So I wait, going through all the motions required of being a good mother, glad to have something to keep me busy.

It is only when I finally put both kids to bed after dinner that I realize that maybe he is not coming back tonight after all.

The night sky is littered with a thousand twinkling stars and I gaze at them from the balcony of my living room on the fifteenth floor. I pace the length of the balcony restlessly. The cool night breeze caresses my cheeks. I walk inside. I continue to wait, engulfed by the darkness in the drawing room, and go sit on the leather armchair where I usually read my morning paper, too afraid to call, too afraid to try to make sense of it all, and too afraid to look, for fear of what I will find as my life hangs in suspension. And as I wait for my husband to come home, my mind races back to that time in my life before I became a wife and a mother, the time when he had first walked into my life and swept me off my feet.

Waiting for Saturday Night

February
2001
Mumbai

When you are twenty-six, slightly plump, and have never been on a date before, a chance date with the office hunk sounds like manna from heaven. Well, it is not really a date, but still, I am going out *alone* with Prashant Mathur to the Taj Hotel, no less.

Prashant—the casanova whom women swoon over and will give an arm and a leg to go out with. And he will be taking *me*, Nisha—the plain Jane. Actually that should be Nisha-the-*plump*-plain-Jane.

Okay, so this is not a *real* date, but it still is the closest that I have come to one.

The travel agency where I am employed has received an invite from Magellan International, one of the big players in the travel industry, for a grand party happening at the Taj hotel. Our agency, Point to Point, is a very minuscule one, small fry in comparison to the big players in the business. All we do is pass on our ticketing requirements to them and they do the bookings for us. We are simply a collection and drop-off point for passports and visa requirement forms. We are not even a proper travel agency in the truest sense of the word, but I absolutely love my office, my job, and my colleagues.

There are just six of us employed here—three men, Prashant, Sanjay, and Akash, and three women, Chetana, Deepti, and me. We don't even have an office peon. And among the men, Prashant is without doubt, a *very* good-looking man. He is nearly six feet tall and slim built, with hair stylishly slicked back. His phone is always ringing off the hook, but he makes himself deliberately 'unavailable' to prying girls through us. At times, he talks in a low voice and we know instantly that he is fixing up a date.

If our measly salaries could afford a mobile phone, I think he would have been on it all the time. But back then, mobile phones were just playthings of the rich, and so we continue taking Prashant's personal calls, making excuses for him when he does not want to talk. Sanjay already has a girlfriend, and as soon as office gets over, he rushes off to meet her. The guys are all on the sales team. Their job is to go out and get business for the agency and file reports at the end of the day. The girls man the counters, which means we mostly answer phone calls and smile sweetly at whosoever comes to the agency. My job may not be the greatest in the world, but it means the world to me. It is my very first job and I landed this after a travel and tourism course. The pay isn't much but I love the sense of belonging I have here. It is also the first time in my life that I am earning my own money, giving me a sense of achievement.

'Hey Nisha, want to grab a cup of coffee?' asks Akash.

'That sounds good. Give me two minutes,' I say, as I note down the booking details of a client.

'I am coming too. I badly need one. Who else is coming?' asks Chetana.

No one responds, so the three of us cross the road to the coffee shop across, which is our usual haunt for breaks. Akash is the youngest amongst us. He is just twenty years old and fresh out of college. But he is smart, clever, and talks well, which is probably the reason why he got the job at Point to Point.

Chetana, with her stylish haircut, flawless complexion, easy laugh, and eyes that twinkle, is easily the best-looking girl in our office. Usually, she is dressed to kill, her wardrobe consisting of mostly short skirts and well-fitted tops. She is from a wealthy family and is just biding her time in this travel agency, as it will give her a chance to tell people that she is 'working', till she gets married. We are all certain she will get married to a wealthy businessman from her community and live in the lap of luxury for the rest of her life, or she will get married to someone from the US and migrate there for good.

Just as we are midway through the coffee, Sanjay calls out from across the road and says, 'Guys, get back! Bulging cover alert,' as we all gulp down our remaining coffee and hurry back to office.

'Bulging cover alert' is our code for our boss, the lady who owns the travel agency. She is a rich, affluent lady by the name of Parinita Sachdev, who mostly comes to office just once a week, clack–clacketying her six-inch heels and looking down upon all of us disdainfully as she walks into her cabin which is almost always kept locked in her absence. She then 'checks accounts' for an hour or so and hands out any communication (usually she carries a huge envelope stuffed with papers, thus earning herself the name 'bulging cover') and walks out as swiftly and smartly as she arrives. She is pencil thin, with a perfect hairdo, perfectly manicured hands, and the looks of a model straight from the pages of *Vogue* magazine. If rumour mills are to be believed, she is the mistress of Jairaj Singhania, one of the co-founders of Singhania Hotels—a large chain of luxury hotels.

Jairaj Singhania is a well-known public figure who makes regular appearances on Page 3 columns in newspapers. Rumours abound that he has bought Parinita Sachdev not just an apartment in Lokhandwala Complex, but also this travel agency, where we all work, to give her something to do, so she can play boss lady and order minions like us around, when he really should be devoting all his time to his hotel industry and his wife and kids.

None of us know if there is any truth in these rumours, but we are inclined to believe them as Parinita seems unbelievably wealthy, and anyone with even half a brain can figure out that a measly little travel agency cannot be her *sole* source of income. She always arrives in a chauffeur-driven Mercedes. The driver almost trips over himself as he rushes to open the door for Her Highness as she climbs out of the car. Even street dogs seem to stand at attention when she arrives.

I shift uneasily in my chair when she arrives, wishing I could somehow smoothen out the layers of fat on my body, which I usually manage to somewhat conceal with clever clothing. But the moment Parinita Sachdev walks in, I feel inadequate.

That morning, she doles out the invite from Magellan International (the one that will change the course of my life, but I am yet to know that), and before she marches out breezily, she says, 'Oh, you all decide amongst yourself, which two will attend this party. I have no interest in it.' She drops the invite like a used tissue on our counter and marches out, leaving a trail of expensive perfume in the air.

As soon as she leaves, all of us eagerly gather around the invite.

'Oh wow! It's at the Taj!' exclaims Deepti.

'Not bad!' says Chetana.

'Let's decide by draw of lots which two get to go,' suggests Akash. Akash is the practical one in the group.

Deepti writes out the guys' names first and when Prashant's name is pulled out, he looks very pleased, as Akash and Sanjay congratulate him.

Next it is the women's turn. I cannot believe my luck when my name is pulled out. I have never won anything before this, not even at those school raffles. But unlike the school raffle tickets, the chances of my name emerging are of course one third here. Still, I never thought I'll get lucky. I am very pleased too, till I steal a quick glance at Prashant's face. He looks positively disgusted now.

I am certain Prashant has been hoping to go with Chetana. To all of us (except Chetana perhaps), on our ridiculously low salaries, a chance to party at a five-star hotel is hard to pass on. But after seeing Prashant scowl,

I have half my mind of passing on my chance to Chetana.

I take her aside and ask her, 'Hey Chetana, do you want to go instead of me? Just look at his face.'

'No, Nisha. Your name has been drawn fair and square. It is really a chance for you. You must go. Just watch me. I know how to handle the likes of Prashant.'

'Hey, Prashant, what is with you? Can't you be a gentleman for once and be nice to Nisha?' she says sweetly to him, in a half-coquettish way.

Her frankness and open confrontation without any animosity takes him completely by surprise, but he quickly recovers. He would have jumped off a mountain cliff if Chetana had asked him to. That was the effect Chetana had on most men.

'Of course, Chetana. I don't mind going out with Nisha,' he answers.

Then he turns towards me and squeezes my arm and says, 'Hey babe, you will have fun. Wear something nice.'

I am shocked and surprised and also very pleased, even though I know he is just obliging Chetana. The excitement in me refuses to die down.

Throughout my way home, I smile in anticipation of attending a party with Prashant Mathur. I live with my father in Parel and I have to travel to Andheri to reach the travel agency in Lokhandwala. That works very well for me, as it works against the maddening rush-hour traffic both times in the local trains of Mumbai; when people are always rushing towards the city, I rush towards the suburbs and so getting here as well as getting back home are easy.

My father does not care in the least bit about my whereabouts. I lost my mother to cancer when I was five and my father never remarried. He instead employed an old lady, whom I fondly called Malati Tayi, to look after me. She passed away when I was sixteen, leaving a gaping hole in my heart. I was too young to have remembered my mother's death. My father, I have been told, changed a lot after my mother's death. I have no memories of how he had been before she died. He had loved her dearly and had done all he could to save her. I have studied her photographs and she is pretty. I think I look a lot like my mother (except that my mother was very slim), and perhaps looking at me is a painful reminder to him of happy memories which he could never have with her. So he mostly left me alone, and I grew into a lonely child, with hardly any friends to play with.

When I first landed the job at this agency, I was ecstatic beyond repair. I have stuck here for four years now, in my mundane little safe existence. I come to work, the hours pass, and I go home. At the end of the month, I get paid, and I deposit my cheque in my bank account.

Akash, Sanjay, Prashant, Chetana, and Deepti are my first 'real friends', although I doubt they consider me so. To them, I am perhaps just 'Nisha—the-slightly-plump-and-pleasant-office-colleague'. I do not really mind though. I am happy to belong somewhere.

The first big event that has happened to me in my uneventful existence of my office life so far is this date. And it has come by a draw of lots! Perhaps there indeed is something called destiny—I do not know, because

I had no idea then that a single date can change one's life.

Whatever it is, I am a really happy girl today. Prashant Mathur has even called me babe, squeezed my hand, and told me to wear something nice. Oh yes, I definitely will!

I count the hours left and can hardly contain my excitement till Saturday, the day of the party.

Luck Be a Lady

Chetana knows what a big deal this date is for me. She has kindly offered to help me dress up for it, graciously opening the contents of her wardrobe to me, and helping me pick out a dress for the party. Her basic plan is to educate me on what kind of clothes can be defined as stylish and what accessories can be teamed up with various outfits. We are in her bedroom with almost twenty outfits of hers casually thrown across the bed.

'Chetana, how in the world do you suppose I'll fit into your outfits? I am so much bigger than you,' I say.

But Chetana says she has many loose-fitting ones from a time when slightly oversized clothes were the rage.

I feel a bit like Audrey Hepburn in *My Fair Lady* before her education and makeover.

'Try this black top,' she says, as she tosses it carelessly at me.

I am not coy and change right in front of her, as she gets busy digging full throttle futher into her wardrobe to scoop out more alternatives.

My breasts are jutting out, leaving the cleavage exposed for all to see. But I have managed to squeeze into the dress and decide that it does not look too bad after all.

Chetana takes out a colourful stole and wraps it stylishly around my neck, which partly covers my breasts and cleavage in a very sexy way.

Then she orders me to try out her six-inch heels. I dutifully oblige.

'Now for some make-up,' she says, as she pulls open my hair which I have tied into a severe ponytail. She ruffles it expertly like a hairdresser who knows her job well and lets it hang loosely over my shoulders. She whips out mascara and an eyelash lengthener. I examine the packaging and notice that it is really expensive. 'Really expensive' here is defined as costing almost as much as my half-month's salary. And it is just a little tube. But I say nothing and go with the flow.

This is the first time I have had someone showing this much interest in me and helping me get dressed, and I decide that I am not going to let a little thing like the price of an eyeliner affect me.

Chetana advises me to wear her wrap-around skirt and I oblige, with the final touch being a pair of six-inch wedge heels which make me look taller and as a consequence, ten pounds lighter. The end result is that 'Nisha-the-plain-Jane' is now transformed into 'Nisha-the-head-turning-babe'. I am stunned at the transformation and I feel a bit like Cinderella going to the ball. But most importantly, I feel desirable.

Then Chetana gives me a small packet containing some pills. I am genuinely puzzled.

'What is this for?' I ask.

'Just in case,' she winks.

I still do not comprehend.

'Just in case of what?'

'Morning-after pill, you silly! Never go unprepared on a date. You never know where it can end.'

I stare at her like she is crazy. How in the world will my first date end up in sex? Chetana really goes overboard sometimes. But just to oblige her, I slip it into my bag.

'You are really crazy!' I say.

Prashant has agreed to meet me at the Andheri station from where we would be taking the Mumbai local to Churchgate. As it is off peak-hours, Prashant says we can travel together in the general compartment. He is right. But I cannot help wishing he had hired a cab instead.

Oh well, whom am I kidding here? I know I am lucky just to be on a date with him.

He looks pleased when he sees me. The scowl which earlier marked his face, is now replaced with lust in his eyes. He lets out an appreciative sigh as he says, 'Glad you decided to wear something good.' Then he looks me up and down and he actually takes my arm.

I am singing and dancing, leaping in joy inside my head, but outwardly I pretend as thought I go on dates like these every day.

The party is in full swing when we arrive. I suddenly feel very important and confident about my outfit and about the fact that I am with an attractive man.

But my elation is short-lived. When I walk inside, the first thing that strikes me is that almost all the men and women look like models here. How can a room contain so many good-looking people? They look stylish and elegant in an understated way. The women are in short, tight, skimpy outfits. Suddenly my borrowed wrap-around skirt and the black top and stole pale in comparison with the designer stuff all these people seem to be sporting.

'Hey, Leena, is that really you? What a pleasant surprise!' says Prashant as he spots a woman with very short hair and a little black dress that barely covers her bottom or her breasts which seem to spill out voluptuously from the top of the outfit. She has a pencil-thin waist. She is holding a drink in one hand and her heavy red lipstick and thick black eyelashes make her look like one of those women from the superhero comics that I read as a child.

Prashant does not even bother introducing me to her. They get busy talking and suddenly Prashant asks her to dance, leaving me all alone. I feel abandoned and I have no idea what to do. I look around and walk towards the table at the far end of the room where food has been laid out for the guests.

I feel truly out of place now and try to hide my discomfort by pretending to appear busy. I walk towards the food counter and keep myself busy raising the steel lids of the rectangular containers placed in a long row with several others containing the food for the party. I am looking at the way the spring rolls have been arranged inside one and at the way the cutlery is laid out.

It is at that exact moment that Samir walks into my life. Of course, I have no idea at that moment that I am talking to my future husband.

'Are you hungry?' he asks with a twinkle in his eye.

I am embarrassed to be caught checking out the food like this.

'Uh…err… not really,' I mutter.

He smiles as his eyes meet mine. He is dressed in a single-breasted tuxedo jacket with a peak lapel. He is tall, could easily be six feet one, and his hair is slicked back stylishly. I notice the cleft on his chin and the dimple in his right cheek as he smiles. My heart does a flip as my eyes meet his. He is very handsome and he seems to be unaware of his looks or charm. He seems straight out of a Mills & Boon novel, which I used to devour as a teenager. Prashant's looks pale in comparison to his.

'How can I let my guest be without a drink? What can I get you?' he asks.

'Well, I'll let you decide,' I say.

'Do you hand over the charge of what you want so easily to others?'

'Only when they are as good-looking as you,' I hear myself saying.

What has come over me? Why am I flirting and throwing myself so darn shamelessly at this guy? Why am I acting like I have never seen a good-looking male before? *Because no man this good-looking has even spoken to you before and you are so flattered with the attention he is giving you.*

'Stop it, Nisha!', I admonish myself inside my head.

He tilts his head and laughs in delight.

'Bold!' he says. 'I like that!' he adds, as he goes off to get me a drink.

'A daiquiri for a charming woman, who is not afraid to let a man take charge,' he says, handing over my drink to me. Then he leads me to one of the tables and we sit down. 'Is your drink fine?' he asks.

I take a sip and I love it.

'Perfect,' I reply.

I am grateful for his company and his unflinching attention towards me. I turn around and try to find Prashant but he is lost somewhere in the crowd. 'So which travel agency are you from?' asks Samir.

'Point to Point in Andheri,' I say.

'Aaah, the one owned by Parinita Sachdev. Jairaj is a friend.'

'Oh!' I say, surprised that he knows them.

Then before I can stop myself, I find myself asking. 'Is it true after all?'

'What is true?' he says, pretending to feign ignorance, watching me squirm and turn a pale shade of red.

Then he chuckles at my visible embarrassment and says, 'Hey, I was just teasing you. They are both very good friends. That's all,' he says.

I quickly change the topic.

'So where do you work?' I ask.

'Shhhhh. Don't tell anybody! It is a secret. I simply pretend to work for Magellan International,' he says.

Suddenly in the background, just behind Samir, I see Prashant standing. He is gesturing wildly at me.

I have no idea what he is saying or trying to say. I decide to ignore him. I turn my attention to my daiquiri and to Samir. Years of studying in a women's college has fine-tuned the efforts needed to turn on the feminine charm. I am going full steam here, laughing at his jokes and making a lot of eye contact with him while the conversation is bubbling as smoothly as the champagne he is sipping.

Serves Prashant right for ignoring me and walking off with Leena!

With Samir paying so much attention to me, I don't feel dowdy anymore. I can't be so bad if Samir is ignoring all the gorgeous women in the party and talking only to *me*.

Then I notice that time and again, his gaze wanders to another woman who is dressed to kill in a red gown with a slit riding right up to her thigh. She is clinging to a guy like he is Spider-man and she is Mary Jane who has just been rescued by him.

'Ex-girlfriend?' I ask Samir directly.

Years of observing people in relationships, without actually being in any, have honed my intuitive abilities.

'Oh my God! Are you a witch?' He sounds astonished.

'In secret, I brew love spells. But mostly they turn into dust instead of lust,' I reply back with a smile.

'Oh, you don't need a spell for lust,' he says, as he looks into his glass for a few seconds.

Then he looks up and suddenly asks me out.

'What are you doing tonight?' he asks.

All the women's magazines have told me that it is never a good idea to say yes to a guy as soon as he asks. But to hell with all that advice. It is the first time in my life a guy has actually asked me, 'Nisha-the-plain-Jane', out. I am not about to blow my chance at a great night by playing hard to get.

'Nothing much. I actually do have quite some free time in hand,' I say.

'Let me take you out to this really lovely place. I'll drop you back home,' he says.

I agree, and that is how I bag my first *real* date.

I excuse myself and he tells me to meet him at the lobby straight after the party. He excuses himself and says he has some work to attend to, and that he will see me later.

I truly wish I could do a handstand and shout like a cheerleader. I cannot believe my luck. This just seems to be getting better and better by the minute.

Then I find Prashant and tell him to go home by himself and that I have a date.

'What?' says Prashant, not believing a word I tell him. He acts as though I've told him to jump off the balcony of the hotel. I could have truly. I do not care. I am so happy and elated about Samir asking me out.

'Whom are you going out on a date with? Samir Sharma?' sniggers Prashant.

'How do you know his full name when even I don't?' I reply.

Prashant's jaw drops to the floor.

'I don't believe this! You really are!' he exclaims.

Then he tells me that Samir is one of the big names at Magellan International and is quite well known in the travel industry. Trade pundits call him one of the 'rising stars'.

It is my turn to be surprised now. What did he see in me? Why has he asked me out?

I do not know. But I sure am about to find out.

Twist of Fate

When my heart was doing a secret merry jig at the prospect of going out on a date with Samir Sharma himself, it would have slowed down its pace had it known a disaster was waiting to occur. It was blissfully unaware as I had no idea what was to follow. I am so excited I can barely think. All I know is that the expression 'over the moon' is making perfect sense to me right now. I am elated, happy, and exuberant, and I do not care at all about anything else in the world.

Samir is waiting in the hotel lobby with a packet in his hand. No sooner than he spots me, he waves enthusiastically and starts walking towards me. He then hands over the packet which I now see is gift wrapped in an attractive-looking red satin paper with a golden bow on top.

'Wow. Thanks!' I say, unable to hide my surprise and obvious joy.

It is the perfect start to a dream date.

'Do I open it now?' I ask.

'No. Later please. There's enough time for that.' He smiles amusedly, and it makes me feel like a petulant child who has asked if the chocolate can be eaten right there and then. He then escorts me to his car.

I am not big on cars and have no idea what make his car is, but I can tell it is one of those very expensive ones. I am overwhelmed by the luxury of it all. I am also overwhelmed by the smell of his very masculine perfume. What has he done? Emptied the whole bottle on himself? It takes all my self-control to refrain from sniffing appreciatively in the air and inhaling the scent deeply. He switches on the music and a sexy, deep, male voice which I fail to recognize, starts crooning.

'Great music! Who is this singer?' I ask.

'Have you never heard of Barry White?' he asks.

I haven't and he proceeds to name a few songs, one of which I recollect having heard but had not known who the singer was.

We drive to an exclusive restaurant in south Mumbai, complete with an indoor garden with large, dense green bamboo foliage, white pebbles, and water bodies. It is all very Zen-like and extremely peaceful. The doorman greets him by his name and the hostess whisks us away to a lovely table in the corner, very discreet and classy. I am completely taken in by Samir's style and elegance.

I go very quiet, slowly absorbing my surroundings.

'Have I managed to cast a spell on you, or is that only your prerogative?' he asks, eyes twinkling again.

'That is something we will have to figure out,' I answer.

We order wine (or rather he orders and I just play along) and some food. The conversation continues to flow easily like before. I have no idea when the evening slips into night. I am enchanted, mesmerized, and completely under his spell. I think if he took out a flute and played it like the Pied Piper, I would have probably followed him like the rats into the river.

It is only when Samir asks me about my family that I remember that I have not told my father where I am. I explain my current living arrangements to Samir, about my mother passing away when I was a child, and tell him that I have to make a call to my father. He whips out his cell phone and asks for my father's number. I tell him and he keys it in, hands over the phone to me, and excuses himself so I can talk in private. I cannot help admiring his sense of good manners and consideration.

I tell my father that something came up at work, so I will be home late, and that a colleague will be dropping me off later. My father is not very concerned and I can't tell if it even registered with him that I wasn't home yet. But I am satisfied, as I have done my bit as a dutiful daughter and informed him of my whereabouts. I end up feeling a little upset about my father being so nonchalant. Does he even care?

When Samir comes back, he senses a slight change in my mood and asks if I want more wine. I noddingly oblige, even though I know I am getting slightly tipsy at having drunk beyond my usual alcohol tolerance levels.

'Stop Nisha, do not get drunk on your first date!' scream the voices from the women's magazines. But I tell them to shut up. They do not have a non-caring father and a mother who died on them when they were five. They do not know what it is to grow up friendless and alone. They have no idea what it is like to be bullied all through childhood. They do not know what it is to get no male attention when you most want it. It is the first time someone has found me fascinating enough to ask me out on a date, and I am determined to squeeze the maximum out of it.

Samir is talking about some of the office parties he attended and all the comical stuff that happens there. I find it hilarious and holler with laughter. He is a good conversationalist. Then I ask him questions about his childhood and he describes how he had grown up in a huge, palatial house in a coffee plantation, how he had been sent to one of India's finest boarding schools, and how much he enjoyed his childhood as well as his school. His adolescence and his life are so different from mine. I ask him about his parents and I come to know that his father is no more, and his mother now lives in the UK with his brother, and that he vacations there for at least a month every year.

I am fascinated by a peep into his world. I ask him about London and other places in Europe, all of which he has travelled to extensively. My only knowledge of these places is from geography textbooks and photos in colourful brochures, with all the attractions that tourist agencies print in order to sell these destinations to prospective clients. Nobody in my circle has travelled abroad ever. I am hearing firsthand what these places are like and am not able to have enough of it.

Finally, it is he who suggests that we should head back home as it is getting increasingly dark. I still do not want this date to end and I can sense that neither does he. But he asks for the bill anyway and I notice him adding a very generous tip. He then says that there is a lovely place near his home which serves some amazing ice cream and asks if I want to go. Of course I do. Anything to get some more time with him.

So we leave and begin walking towards his car. I stride to the edge of the pavement and suddenly my heel trips over an uneven surface, making me fall over and go crashing to the ground. As I fall, my forehead bangs against a telephone pole and the impact doubles. One minute I am walking and the other minute, everything goes blank and I am in excruciating pain. I feel so darn embarrassed. But despite the pain, I yank my wrap-around skirt in a hurried attempt to cover my thighs and salvage some of my dignity, totally horrified that this has happened in front of Samir. I just hope he hasn't seen my underwear flashing.

He is standing beside me, looking worried and saying, 'Oh my God, are you okay?'

My forehead is throbbing with a stabbing pain, but I manage a weak smile.

'Oh no! You're bleeding. Let us get you to a hospital,' says a concerned-looking Samir helping me up.

As I stand up, I notice to my utter horror that my skirt (or rather Chetana's skirt) is ripped beyond repair. My right leg is bleeding profusely. I can't even look at Samir. I have never felt this mortified in my entire life. I somehow want to redeem the situation. What must Samir be thinking of me? That I cannot hold a drink and my balance? God!

'No, no, I am fine. Just a little shaken. I don't want to go to a hospital,' I assert firmly.

He nods meekly and as we get into the car, I take out my handkerchief and dab my leg. I don't want to bleed all over his car and spoil his car seats.

'Look, it's late in the night, and I live close by. It will take us at least an hour to get to your place from here. The wiser thing would be to go to my place if you don't mind,' he suggests.

And that is how I end up spending the night in Samir's apartment which is no less than a penthouse, situated in one of the most upmarket areas of south Mumbai. It is ridiculously luxurious and like nothing I have seen before. It even has a circular skylight over the foyer and offers a spectacular view of the millions of twinkling stars that adorn the night sky.

Samir guides me to the guest bedroom and I have to stop myself from gasping at the opulence of the mansion.

He walks to the bathroom and comes out with a bottle of antiseptic and some cotton.

'Let me fix that nasty wound,' he says.

'No really, I am fine. I'll do it,' I insist. It comes out louder than I intended, and I hope that I do not sound like a shrieking witch to him.

Samir looks at me uncertainly.

'Are you sure?' he asks.

'Positive.'

'Okay, I'll leave you to retire then. Everything you need—toothbrush, toothpaste, soap—it's all there.'

'Thanks.'

'There's also a dressing gown in the closet. It's not your size, I am afraid. But I don't have anything else.'

I just want him to go out. I want to nurse my wound and my battered ego. By myself.

'Goodnight, and I am so sorry about this.'

'Please don't be. It's fine really. Am glad about the company and the nice time we had,' he says, as he walks out and closes the door behind him.

I rush to the bathroom and check out my face. There is an ugly bruise on my forehead.

I clean up my leg which has stopped bleeding now but still stings from the antiseptic I had applied a while ago.

What a horrendous end to the perfect dream date.

I look at my surroundings. The bathroom is so posh and luxurious that I take a tissue and clean the counter of the few drops of water that splashed outside the wash basin when I washed my face.

I change into his dressing gown and wrap it around myself. It feels so strange. This is the first time in my life that I have worn a piece of man's clothing. It feels so weirdly intimate. Despite my earlier embarrassment and horror at landing in such a silly situation, I begin to relax. My thudding heart finally begins to calm. All this while I was floating in air, suspended out of reality by Samir's presence on me. But the fall has brought me crashing down to earth. Literally and figuratively.

I think of Chetana's torn skirt and her top that now has dirt streaks all over it. I feel worse about the torn skirt than my bleeding leg. I just hope the skirt wasn't too expensive. I also think about my dad and whether he will even notice I wasn't home. Then I think of work and realize that I have to be at office the next day.

There is a tiny alarm clock beside the bed. I set it for 5 a.m. I want to be up much before Samir wakes up. I want to look fresh, and most importantly, I want to be on time for office. I would not have been so eager had I known what was to follow.

But I do not know it then. And so, finally, I slip into the land of slumber, surrounded by luxury in an attractive guy's apartment, a guy I just met for the very first time. Under different circumstances, I would have been thrilled about it. But right now, I just want to get back to my normal life, as soon as possible.

All Nightmare Long

I am up long before the alarm clock rings. The events of the previous evening all come rushing back to me, and the scenes replay themselves inside my head once more. It feels unreal, almost like a rerun of a well-known movie played many times on television, and yet you cannot help watching it, even though you have seen it all before and even know the dialogues by heart. My toes curl in embarrassment recalling last night's happenings and now I am certain I do not want to see Samir's face again. I decide to quietly leave. If I leave right now, there will still be enough time to go home, have a change of clothes, and then travel to work.

I wear the same outfit from the previous night, adjusting the skirt in such a way that the tear comes at the side. I look into the full-sized mirror and study my reflection as I hang my handbag over my left shoulder so that it conceals the tear. I moisten my hands with water and try to brush away the dirt streaks from Chetana's black top. There—it looks passable now and I am sure people will not stare. Then I look for a pen and paper to leave Samir a note.

I rummage through his bedside drawer and find a pair of long, intricate silver earrings. Beautifully carved, the shining stone set in its middle looks like a diamond. Somehow I find my heart getting heavier.

Don't be ridiculous, Nisha, you hardly know the guy. He must have slept with dozens of women and you must simply be a new distraction for him.

I know its plain silly of me to feel bad about finding a pair of earrings in his spare bedroom, but I cannot help it.

God—what is wrong with me? First I throw myself at him, then I ruin a wonderful evening by tripping and falling down, and now I am fretting over a pair of earrings.

I hurriedly shut the drawer and slowly tiptoe out of the bedroom. I am relieved to find that he is nowhere in sight. I let myself out, carrying my heels in one hand, so that the click-clack of their noise when I walk in them does not wake him. I stealthily creep out like a burglar, and only once outside, do I finally wear my heels. Then I close the door which clicks automatically shut. I check to see if it opens from the outside, and when it doesn't, I go downstairs into the street and hail a cab.

At my home, my father has hardly noticed my last night's absence, or even if he had, he has chosen to say nothing about it. It suits me fine as it is the last thing I want to talk about.

On my entire journey to my workplace, I keep thinking of how I have gone out with two attractive men in a single day, and what a difference there is in both their attitudes. Prashant had taken me to an office party in a

Mumbai local train while Samir had taken me to an ultra-posh place in an ultra-posh car. But then again, Prashant had been kind of forced to go with me, while Samir seemed to have genuinely enjoyed my company. Yet I cannot help feeling a little bit of resentment towards Prashant. I am not that uninteresting for him to have been so callous. More than callous, he has taken me for granted, and I am a bit angry at him for having treated me so. I decide that if ever a situation like this arises in the future (which I am certain will not happen as this was an entirely one-off thing), I am definitely not going out with Prashant again. He can chase the Leenas of the world. I am okay without a date. I have had enough of being treated shabbily.

I reach work on time, freshly showered and looking much more bright and chirpy than I feel inside. I am certain that I do not want to tell anybody about last night's date with Samir. I do not want Chetana and the rest of the gang at work to know. I feel lousy about it anyway, and reliving it all over again will only propound my misery. Surely if I brush it aside and pretend it was nothing, they will probably forget about it? In a few days, all of this will be history. That is the grand plan I make on 'How to deal with the Samir disaster'.

But when I reach office, I cannot escape the questions. Chetana is waiting to pounce on me.

'Halooo madam! Bright and happy! How went everything?' she asks and winks.

I see Prashant perking up his ears and waiting for my reply. I know instantly that he has told everybody at office that I went on a date with Samir Sharma himself.

'Oh, nothing to write home about. It was okay,' I mutter, pretending to get busy by opening a file.

'Come on, woman, spill the beans! Don't act so snobbish just because you went out with Samir,' persists Chetana.

Prashant has now stopped pretending to be interested and has walked over to the counter and is resting his face in his elbows.

There is a slight sneer in his voice as he says, 'Yeah, yeah, go on and share with us what you *did* last night.'

I am irked now with Prashant's needling and his 'I-am-God's-gift-to-womankind' attitude. I am angry with him for being so condescending. I am indignant at the shabby way he has treated me so far and after last night's events, my blood now boils thinking about the way he walked off with Leena, without even so much as bothering to talk to me. The whole Samir fiasco would not have happened had Prashant stayed by my side. But there is no way I am letting him know it has affected me even the least bit. And now he has the bloody cheek to taunt me, asking me with a sneer, what I *did*!

'Actually,' I say, and I pause for effect, 'I spent the night at his apartment.'

'You what?!!' exclaim both Prashant and Chetana in utter shock, as though I have dropped hot coals on them. I, of course, do not bother to explain the circumstances under which I spent the night.

I flash a triumphant smile at Prashant. I want to rub his nose in some more.

'And Samir happens to be good friends with Jairaj

Singhania too,' I add. It feels great and important dropping names.

'Oh my God! Did Samir tell you all this?!' asks Prashant and I can see he is totally impressed. He is not even making an effort to hide it. I feel the slow satisfaction of vengeance further giving a boost to my bruised ego. I feel powerful to see the effect my words are having on him.

'Yes he did, and he told me about Parinita and Jairaj too,' I add in a slightly superior, all-knowing tone.

I can see that suddenly, I have everybody's complete attention. They have stopped doing whatever they were doing and are clearly tuned in to what I have to say. Uh-oh. This has gone beyond the impact I intended it to have. Now I want to take back what I said.

But they are all waiting, as though it is a public-speaking event and I have been given the mike.

I don't know what to do. I can feel my face turning slightly hot. I have said more than I intended to. Now, I desperately look for an escape route.

'So go on then, tell us!' urges Chetana, her eyes full of anticipation at a juicy piece of gossip.

'Oh well, it is nothing really,' I say lamely, wanting the earth to swallow me up.

'So is she his mistress then?' asks Prashant.

Before I can answer, there is a sharp rap on the counter.

We all freeze in horror as we see Parinita Sachdev standing there, like a chiselled marble-stone statue. Her eyes are blazing. Her face is a mask of cold rage and fury.

I feel my hands going icy cold. I am certain she has heard all of our conversation, even though I have no idea how long she has been standing there. We had been so engrossed in our squabbles that we hadn't noticed her coming.

I swallow once and look down, busying myself with reading a letter.

Parinita says nothing and marches into her cabin. I feel my whole body sagging with relief. Everyone scuttles back into their seats and get busy working. Deepti goes into Parinita's cabin to apprise her of the weekly happenings.

After twenty minutes, I find Deepti standing at my counter.

'She wants to see you inside,' she says curtly.

'Did she say why?' I ask, my heart sinking. Parinita has never called me inside before. It is always Deepti who submits the weekly accounts and Prashant submits the reports of their field trips.

I wish now I had kept my mouth shut. I am a silly, immature blabbermouth. I bagged one measly date which went horribly wrong, and I covered up by boasting and pretending to be superior.

I walk into her cabin, my heart thudding hard.

Parinita's face is a mask of ice now. She looks like the white witch straight out from The Chronicles of Narnia.

'Nisha, you can gather your belongings and leave,' she says simply.

It takes me a few seconds to comprehend what she is saying. Then I realize I am being fired.

I open my mouth to speak but no words come out.

Finally, I say weakly, 'But Ma'am, I have worked here for the past four years.'

'You are inefficient, lazy, and do not know how to conduct yourself at an office party. You are a disgrace and have spoiled the image of Point to Point. Now get out of my sight and come to the office at the end of this month to settle your dues,' she spits out the words with venom.

I am shocked and silent. I have always prided myself on doing my work efficiently, on being punctual, and on getting along well with my colleagues. This job is the only one I have had. For the first time in my life, I had felt I belonged somewhere. But now it feels like someone has punched me in the face as a reward for my loyalty.

I walk out quietly, shoulders slumped. I want to protest at the way I have been asked to go. I want to say something in my defence. But words fail me. There is no higher authority to appeal to. Parinita runs the show and her call is final.

I sit at my desk and there is complete silence in the office. Everybody seems to have sensed what has happened. Either that, or Deepti has probably told them. I quietly gather a few personal items lying on my desk. I can feel tears stinging my eyes and I blink them back.

'What happened? What did she say?' whispers Chetana.

But there is a lump in my throat and I do not trust myself to speak. I do not want to start crying in front of everybody and make an unnecessary scene.

I simply nod and do not meet her eyes.

I stuff my things in my bags and make a hasty exit.

'Hey, you okay?' asks Akash, as I head towards the exit door.

I just nod and pull out my sunglasses, wearing them on my way out.

It is only when I am seated in the local train that I remember I have not returned Chetana's clothes.

I feel miserable and Parinita's words keep going round and round in my head. I am definitely not inefficient as she said. I have the urge to go back and scream at her. But I do not have the guts to face her. I hate my cowardice. I hate the fact that I have said nothing in my defence. I hate how meekly I have behaved and quietly accepted her hurled abuses.

I was perfectly content yesterday morning, when I was going on a date with Prashant. I was over the moon when Samir asked me out.

And now there is no Prashant, no Samir, no Point to Point. I have nothing to look forward to from tomorrow. Why tomorrow; from right now itself. I have no job, no identity, and I really do not know what to do, as I sit in the train, feeling leaden, feeling blue, and wishing and wishing I had kept my big mouth shut.

The only life I knew, and was leading, has come to an abrupt end and there is nothing I can do about it.

Some You Win, Some You Lose

'Not getting ready for office today?' asks my father, peering over his glasses from above the newspaper.

'I have taken a week off. Just wanted to take a break,' I lie.

He just shakes his head and busies himself with reading the newspaper, after which he leaves for work. He has worked in the same organization in Vikhroli for the past thirty years, and words like 'taking a break' do not exist in his vocabulary. In fact, people tell me that he went right back to work the next day of my mother's funeral. Perhaps that is the only way he knows to prevent his grief from spilling all over and making a mess of his life.

But I do not have that option, and so I sit down and cry. Large sobs. Like a child whose favourite toy is broken. I feel sorry for myself. After about fifteen minutes of crying, I realize that nobody is going to help me but myself. The crying has given me some emotional release and I go and wash my face and brew myself a cup of tea.

Then I take the newspaper and start circling the classified jobs. I have narrowed down three after making several phone calls. I have an interview in the afternoon the same day and I have two more lined up for tomorrow.

Ultimately, all of them turn out to be dead leads. For the first one, all they want is a typist, even though the position advertised had said front office manager. As it turns out, there isn't much of a front or much of an office either. The other interview has a fat, bespectacled, middle-aged guy wearing a dhoti and a Gandhi cap, chewing paan, and as he spits out he asks if I am willing to deposit all my original degree certificates for two years with them as a 'bond' or a guarantee that I will not quit for the next two years. I am very uncomfortable at the prospect of being chained to an organization like that, and so I refuse. The third interview has a lecherous old bastard who talks more to my breasts than to me. I can actually see him drooling and eyeing me lasciviously which makes me feel all creepy. He does not take his eyes off my cleavage the whole time, his eyes almost popping out like a toad. I run out in terror, even as he offers to raise my pay.

Seven more days (and eleven more interviews) of similar kind follow. I call, I set up interviews, I attend them with hope, but mostly what they advertise isn't what they really want. By the end of the seventh day, I am tired and frustrated. I feel dumb and worthless. My diploma in travel and tourism does not seem to count much in all the jobs that I am applying for. But then, hardly any travel agencies advertise for their staff positions. Recruitments in the travel industry are done mostly through word of mouth or through campus recruitments (which was how I had landed the job at Point to Point, fresh out of college).

I curse stupid Parinita and her precious Jairaj. I truly do not care whether she is his mistress or madame. I curse Prashant. I curse my big mouth for having boasted about my stupid date. All I want is a decent job. But I do not seem to be able to manage even that.

The prospect of sitting at home with nothing to do scares me to death. I am at my wits end and am fast losing my patience too. I truly do not know what to do except wait for the next day's paper, in the faint, tiny hope that some travel agency in some obscure corner of Mumbai might need a travel assistant like me. Apart from the eleven interviews that I have attended, I have also submitted my CV to many places, where they said they would get back to me after the initial assessment is done.

When the phone rings, I almost jump out of my skin. My heart pounding, I pick it up. It might be someone offering me a job. But it turns out to be Chetana.

'So finally someone remembered that I exist,' I say acidly when she asks how I am, the events of the last few days not helping a great deal to up my mood.

'Hey, look. I am so sorry about not calling earlier, but I was caught up in this whole "arranged marriage" business. My parents just can't seem to leave me alone.'

'Anything clicked? Do we hear wedding bells soon?' I perk up a little despite my current state of misery.

'Arre yaar, the guy looks like a cross between a bull and a bull dog. His nostrils are so big, and by the looks of it, he weighs at least ninety kilos on a five-foot ten-inch frame. Plus the guy seems to know nothing apart from his work, which I know nothing about.'

I giggle at her description of him.

'What made your parents consider him then?' I ask.

'Oh that's easy to guess. His IIT-IIM tag,' she spits out the words and I can almost picture her disgust.

I sigh.

'But hey, listen, that is not why I called! Guess why I did!' she says in a sing-song manner, her voice taking a more upbeat tone now.

'Ummm...does Parinita want me to come back?' I barely whisper, hoping against hope that it is true, hating myself as soon as I say it. If I had any shred of self-respect left, I would not even hope for this outcome, and instead would tell Parinita to stuff her job up her pert you-know-what.

But seven days of useless job hunting has worn down my pride as well as chipped away at my determination. I am ready to beg, borrow, or even steal, as I am desperate for a job like the one I had.

'I wish I could tell you that, but this is something even better,' says Chetana.

Eh?! What can be better than that? I am dying of curiosity now.

'Tell woman! Tell me fast before I explode!' I exclaim.

'Samir called up here a little while ago asking for you!' she says, as though she has delivered a bit of news that will make me want to throw my hands up in a dance.

But to me it is disaster. Oh no! Now Samir would now know that I lost my job. What a shame!

'Oh,' I say unable to hide my disappointment.

'And when Deepti told him that you are no longer working with us, he wanted to know why. She said she had no idea and that you had left.'

'Thank Lord she had that much grace, I mutter.

'But aren't you happy?! Samir Sharma himself actually called up asking for you! He *wants* to talk to you. I would be over the moon if I were you,' says Chetana.

How can I make Chetana understand how much a job means to me at this point in my life? Chetana comes from an affluent family, and she has all the love and acceptance as well as plenty of money. For her, the job at Point to Point is just a temporary thing to occupy herself with, till the time she nets a good husband.

For me, it is everything. It is where I get my acceptance, it is my little secure world, it is where I get my financial independence—as small as it may be. Heck, it is the only place I ever felt I belonged.

I tell Chetana about the last seven days and how unsuccessful I have been at scouting a job for myself.

She does not know what to say.

'Don't worry. Something will turn up,' she finally says to perk me up a little.

Then I remember her soiled clothes and apologize profusely for the tear in her skirt. She asks me to forget about it. She says she doesn't even need them as they do not even fit her anymore. I do not know whether to feel pleased that I was feeling bad about damaging them for nothing or whether to feel upset that I had been handed over discarded clothes which she did not even care about and I had taken great pride in wearing.

Anyway, it is too late to brood about it now, and I have the more pressing matter of finding a job. So I politely thank her and hang up.

The phone rings again almost immediately, startling me again and I pick it up at once and say a resigned hello.

'Hey. Do you always answer on the first ring?' asks a deep voice and it is unmistakably Samir's.

'Oh! It's you. How did you get my number? Did Deepti give it to you?' I ask, quite taken aback that he has called me at home. I never gave him my home number and I did not even think that our paths would cross again, ever.

'Deepti who?' he asks, and I can picture him furrowing his brows.

'Deepti, my colleague at Point to Point,' I say, and as soon as I say it, I realize she is an ex-colleague now. The realization and talking to Samir bring a fresh wave of pain, like a nasty gash which you think is healing, opens up suddenly and spouts blood everywhere.

'Oh no. I have no idea who it was I spoke to there, but I can see you are well informed about my activities,' he teases.

It irks me, even though I know he means it purely as a joke. The last thing I want to do is track the activities of the likes of Samir Sharma. All that is on my mind right now is landing myself a job.

'Look Samir, I have to go. But I would appreciate it if you tell me how you got my home number,' I say a little icily.

'Hey sorry! I didn't mean to annoy you. You had

dialled your dad that day from my cell phone in the restaurant, remember?' he says.

I had almost forgotten about that magical evening which had later turned into disaster. I soften a bit at the memory. Even though it has only been a week, so much has happened since that first date that it feels like a month.

'Oh yes, I do remember,' I say.

And before I can say anything more, Samir has asked me out again. He says he would really like to talk to me about something important and asks if we can go out this Friday, which is tomorrow. I cannot believe it.

One part of me does remember the grand time I had with him. But the other part of me wants to hang my head in shame, after the first disaster of falling flat on the ground in front of him in such an undignified manner. Plus, I'm now without a job and feel too ashamed to tell him I was fired.

'I happen to be in your part of town tomorrow evening, and there is a new place owned by a good friend which is being inaugurated tomorrow. All the A-list celebrities will be there and I find these dos boring. But my chore becomes a lot easier if you agree to go with me,' he persuades.

I still hesitate, but mentally I am thinking that it would be better than sitting at home gloomily, doing nothing on a Friday evening. I have had a really hard week and here is a guy actually asking me out and telling me he enjoyed my company.

'And we can slip out as soon as the ribbon is cut, go somewhere quiet, you know?' he persuades even more, as he senses my hesitation.

That does it. Here is a fun opportunity being handed to me on a platter. All I have to do is put the past behind me and say a yes. I do.

'Oh great then. I'll see you tomorrow. Pick you up at eight then?' he says.

I am horrified at the thought of Samir coming home, that too in his fancy car! So I tell him that I will meet him at a place close to my house. And he agrees.

Then I realize that I again have nothing suitable to wear other than Chetana's discarded clothes. But now I know that I can look good with the right clothes and accessories. There is no way in hell I am again borrowing clothes from Chetana. So I rush to the bank and withdraw the whole of my last month's salary. I save almost all of it, as I live with my dad, and so my food and accommodation is already taken care of. So I do have a tiny fortune carefully squirrelled away over the years.

I realize that I don't even know where to go shopping, other than Fashion Street. Somehow I don't want to wear tacky Fashion-Street imitations and so I make a quick call to Chetana and apprise her of the new situation I am finding myself in,

'You lucky cow,' she almost shrieks when I tell her. 'Fancy Mr Sharma chasing you!' she says.

'Hold on! He just happens to be this side of town. It is not that he is coming here especially for me. Besides, he is just using me as a toy to make his time at the party more bearable. I must just be an amusement for him,' I quickly say. I am not a fool and I can see reality for what it is.

'Don't be such a pessimist, Nisha! He wouldn't have

asked you out a second time, had he not enjoyed your company.'

Maybe she has a point there. But I really do not want to dwell too much on it. I ask her to tell me where I should shop and mentally make a note of her suggestions.

Five hours and three thousand five hundred bucks later, I am back home with a whole new wardrobe and a whole new look.

This is the first time I am actually feeling good ever since the day I lost my job. It makes me feel like I have something to look forward to once more.

And as I try out the different outfits and heels that I just acquired one after the other, posing happily in front of the mirror, I feel quite pleased with my transformation. For the first time I also understand why women call shopping therapeutic.

Once again, I can't wait to meet Samir, and this time I am determined to make it a grand success and not fall flat on my face like I did the last time around.

The Unnamed Feeling

We slip out of the party in exactly ten minutes like he promised. He looks even more handsome than the last time I saw him. He looks so gorgeous that I have to forcibly tear my eyes off him. I am happy that I agreed to accompany him. Last week's events have seriously created a large dent in my self-esteem and Samir treating me like I am really interesting pleases me no end, although the little, niggling voice in my subconscious mind does scream that he is just amusing himself with me. Whatever it is, I am now out with him, and I am determined to have a good time. I don't often get such opportunities.

The party turns out to be a grand affair. Living in Mumbai, one does get used to seeing celebrities every once in a while. After all, this is the mecca of Bollywood. But this is the first time I see so many up close and am able to recognize quite a few. I am not really in awe of them, but I do feel like I have stepped into some television show or a film set. I am suddenly glad that I splurged on my fancy clothes. No longer do I feel like 'Nisha-plain-Jane-in-borrowed-clothes'.

Samir introduces me to his friend whose restaurant is being inaugurated, congratulates him, and poses for a few photographs which he wants me to join in, but I mouth a no, quietly fading into the background. After the pictures are clicked, Samir whispers something to his friend and gestures for me to join them. Then he quickly excuses himself and me. As we slip away, he smiles at me and says, 'There, that wasn't too bad, was it? Hope you weren't too bored.'

'This is the first time I am seeing so many celebrities up close,' I confess.

'It's such a fake world,' he says, his expression darkening slightly. He offers no more explanation and I don't ask either, as we make our way towards his car.

The music that he is playing is an eclectic mix of strange names that I have never heard before. It is soothing and calming. When I ask him what it is, he says he picked it up in one of his favourite haunts in Bali. He asks me if I have ever been to Bali. I say with a little laugh that I have never been outside the country, let alone to an exotic destination like Bali. His world and my world are truly poles apart and I don't think he has a clue. But he is nice enough to not show his surprise and he says, 'Oh, it is a lovely place. You should go sometime,' and I nod and say I must, secretly smiling to myself, thinking that if it was that easy, I'd have visited Bali and many more destinations some fifty times by now.

This time, Samir drives us to a lovely little cafe that overlooks the sea. Again it is tastefully done, discreet and very exclusive. I can't help thinking that he does know some great places in Mumbai. Of course, he has the money to splurge on them too.

When we are comfortably seated, he asks, 'So did you like the songs?'

'You mean the music you just played in the car? I loved it.'

'No, no, I meant the CD I gifted you the last time we met.'

It is only then I remember that I had rushed out of his place without leaving him a note, and that he had gifted me a little something that I had not even opened and which was still lying in a drawer at home. How could I have forgotten?!

'Oh my God, Samir, I am so sorry. I forgot all about it. I haven't even opened it,' I say sheepishly, a little embarrassed now. Samir throws his head back and laughs.

'You are so honest, Nisha! I like that about you,' he says.

I squirm as I think about how my 'honesty' got me thrown out of my last job. But I smile and say nothing.

Samir bowls me a googly just then.

'Nisha, I need to confess something,' he says.

My heart starts beating like the drumbeats of a death metal band. What is he going to confess now? That he fancies me? Is Chetana right after all? It seems impossible to believe. I clench my fists under the table and try my best to appear cool.

'Yes, go on,' I say, trying my best to conceal my trepidation.

'Well, I called up Point to Point, and when they told me you left, I made a call to Parinita.'

I am horrified now. The one thing that I did not want Samir to know was that I had been *thrown* out. In case he asked about my job, I had been planning to tell him the same thing that I had told my dad, that I was simply taking a break. Well, searching for a new job does count as a break, doesn't it?

'Oh,' I say and I feel the colour rising to my cheeks. I realize that Parinita might have told him the whole story of my conversation with my colleagues that day. I am dying to know what she told him and how much he knows. But I am too terrified to ask.

'She really did not tell me the whole story. But from what I gathered, I do think she has been harsh, and when I questioned her as to the exact details, she got irked and implied that how she dealt with her employees was none of my business,' he says, as though he has just read my mind.

I swallow twice and then I say nothing.

'Look Nisha, I am really sorry about what happened and I think I am partly responsible for this,' he continues.

'No Samir, it really isn't your fault,' I finally manage to say.

It truly isn't. I am too shamefaced to confess to him that it was my big mouth and my petty need to rub Prashant's nose in the dirt that made me lose my job.

'Well, I somehow feel responsible, Nisha, and please allow me to make amends. How would you like to work at Magellan International as an Executive Assistant to the senior partner?' he asks.

I cannot believe what I have just heard. Is Samir really offering me a job?! That too at Magellan? And not just at the ticketing desk but as an Executive Assistant! This must be my lucky day!

Samir mistakes my utter shock and disbelief to be disinterest on my part.

'Hey, there is no compulsion to take it up. The person working right now is serving her notice period. She quit as her husband has moved abroad and she is expecting, and we do need someone with a travel agency background to fill up the position. But I completely understand if you have other plans,' he says.

It takes all my self-control to not jump up and down right there and shout out that I will take the job.

'No, I am definitely open to it,' I say. Secretly I am dancing. I am thrilled.

'Oh, that's great then. Just call up the office and ask to speak to Smriti. She will brief you about everything, including the pay and other details. See if it suits you,' he says.

Oh it would suit me all right! Samir has no idea how desperate I am for a job and how hard the last week has been. But of course I tell him none of that, and instead say that I will contact Smriti.

The rest of the date goes off as smooth as silk gliding across marble.

When I get home, I get a call from Akash. He asks me how I am doing and says he misses me at Point to Point. I tell him that I do miss working there and also tell him how unsuccessful I have been in my job hunt, and how finally I have now got a chance at Magellan.

He is genuinely happy for me and wishes me all the best and asks me to keep in touch.

I want to call up Smriti right then. But that would seem too eager, and so I wait until eleven the next morning. The original plan was to wait till evening, but I cannot control myself, and so I make the call.

Smriti is friendly and says she was expecting my call. She says that Samir had spoken to her and she knew I would call. She asks a few quick questions about where I studied, what my diploma is on, and how much work experience I have so far. She asks nothing about my previous job. I am guessing that Samir might have briefed her and asked her not to.

Then she gives me a brief job description and lists out what I am expected to do. It sounds nothing like my boring desk job at Point to Point. Even though I have no experience at the entire job, I am quite confident that I can do it. I am supposed to be coordinating with the senior partner and generally organize all his schedules and appointments. I am also expected to handle the mundane office correspondence. She also says I have to screen visitors, handle communications, and coordinate with various departments in the organization, take care of travel arrangements, hotel bookings, flight bookings, as well as arrange for airport transfers and car rentals, track other tasks, and also handle important visitors as part of my duties. In short, I have to be like a right hand to the senior partner. She asks if I would be able to handle it all. She says the person from whom I am taking over would train me for two days. I answer that I am quite confident of being able to do it. It sounds exciting.

Also, this is *real* work, not just passing on bookings like I did at Point to Point. Here, I would actually be responsible for so many things. I do a double take when I hear what my pay would be. It is three times the amount I have been earning at Point to Point! I truly can dance now. Smriti says they need a person urgently and asks when I can join. I tell her that I can join immediately and she sounds pleased with that. She says she will inform Latha, the lady serving the notice period. She also asks me to come in the next day at 9.30 a.m. sharp and asks me not to be late. Of course I won't! She has no idea how much this job offer means to me.

Then she asks me if I have any questions. I cannot think of any questions at this point, but then it occurs to me that I don't even know who the senior partner to whom I will be Executive Assistant to is.

So I ask Smriti for the name of the senior partner point blank.

There is a surprised silence at the other end.

Then she says, 'Oh! I thought you knew. The senior partner is Samir.'

It is only then that the realization comes whooshing down on me like an unexpected shower of rain on a very hot summer's day. I had no idea I would be reporting to Samir. Somehow, I had presumed that senior partner meant some old guy in the organization and not the charming and suave Samir.

On the one hand I am pleased about it. But on the other hand, I must be the only employee in the world who has dated her boss-to-be, and even spent a night at his home, not to mention fallen down undignifiedly in front of him, flashing her underwear, all this even before she has started working. But still, all this is not reason enough to turn down such a fabulous offer.

Especially when I have no other offers in hand.

I mutter that I will be there on time tomorrow and hang up.

When I lie down that night, it takes me a long while to fall asleep. I am filled with excitement and trepidation, and I feel something in my life is about to change, and it is not just a change of job. I feel that this is a life-altering decision, but at this point, I just cannot put a finger on what exactly it is.

Happily Unhappy

Next morning when I walk into the offices of Magellan International to report for my new job, I feel on top of the world. I finally have a *real* job. I am eager to start, and I am very eager to prove to Samir that I am efficient at my work. I reach the office well on time and go to meet Smriti.

She takes me around the premises. It is nothing like the tiny, cramped space at Point to Point. This is a *real* office, spread across thirty thousand square feet over two floors and employing more than two hundred people.

Smriti tells me that the average age of the employees would be about twenty-six or twenty-seven. It is indeed a young crowd with a lot of parties and fun stuff that happens every Friday evening at the work place itself. She shows me the cafeteria (the most important place she says and winks), the water coolers, the coffee-and-tea-vending machines, and the toilets. I slowly absorb my surroundings and throw a casual glance at all the employees. They are completely absorbed in their work. They do *real* work here, not merely pass on the bookings. I feel very proud to be a part of it all. Smriti takes me around and introduces me to everyone on the floor with whom I would be interacting. I smile pleasantly as they look up from whatever they were busy with and make small talk with them. They respond back jovially. This is a young, friendly bunch and I instantly feel comfortable with them. Ashok, Julie, Divya, Kamal, Nitin, and Mihir—all their names spinning around in my head, as I try to remember their faces and names.

Then I stop dead in my tracks when she introduces me to the next person. It is Leena, the gorgeous woman whom Prashant had walked off with in the party.

'Hi,' she says and then she frowns, 'I have seen you somewhere but I don't recall where,'

'Yeah, we met at the Magellan party. I was with Prashant,' I say dryly.

'Oh yes, I remember now,' she says curtly.

I force a smile, and as soon as my back is turned, I see her making a phone call. I intuitively know through her hushed whispers that she must be calling up Prashant to inform him about my recruitment. Somehow this irks me. But I say nothing, and the rest of the day flies by as Latha briefs me and takes me through all that she has been doing. I am very interested and fascinated with the scope and details of my new job and don't even feel the hours pass. At Point to Point, I would stare at the wall clock all day, waiting for the shift to end. I would leave at 5.30 p.m. sharp to catch the local at 5.42. But here at Magellan, it is already 6.30 p.m., and I have not even realized it.

Samir is travelling abroad and would be back only a week later, she informs me, by which time, I should have settled well into the job. She tells me that I can speak to her if I have any doubts or queries and says that she is happy that I am taking over immediately.

'It is so difficult to work with this,' she adds, as she flops down wearily into an armchair, pointing to her huge belly which looks like it will explode any moment. I feel a little sorry for her and assure her that I will be okay.

In four days, I have eased very well into my new role and feel so much at home—as though I have been working here for ages. My cubicle faces his cabin, and I ought to be able to get a clear view of him when the blinds are pulled up.

When Samir returns, the first thing he does is greet me with a 'Hey Nisha! Good to see you settled here. Come on right in.'

Smriti smiles at me knowingly and winks as I walk into his cabin.

He asks me if there is anything at all that I need, or whether there is any clarification that I want regarding my job. I tell him that Latha has briefed me well and I have been checking with her about a few doubts that I have.

'That's great then!' he says.

I tell him that I have drafted replies to almost all the routine correspondence, and I want him to go through it once to see if my replies are okay, before I send them out. I assure him that this is a one-off thing and I would be handling it on my own once this is approved by him.

He laughs as I reiterate this and says, 'Relax, Nisha, I know you are efficient. Why else do you think I offered you the job in the first place?'

I smile then and know I am going to really enjoy my time here.

In a month's time, it feels as though Samir and I have been working together as a team forever. I badly want to prove myself, making sure I take care of every single thing. I organize his appointments, schedule his meetings, handle routine correspondence, screen his phone calls and visitors, and also give him my inputs on important projects that Magellan is considering when he asks for them. I even see to it that his coffee is kept ready just before his arrival and is just the way he likes it. I, for the first time in my life, am thoroughly enjoying my job and feeling valued. Besides, I am also getting paid well for it. And having an attractive and understanding boss like Samir is truly the cherry on the cake with an already rich icing. He says he cannot understand how in the world he managed before me, and that I have made myself indispensable to his professional life. He says he wants to be able to reach me anytime, for which he gets me a brand new cell phone. It is my first ever, and I am so darn proud of it, as cell phones have just made their entry into India and not everyone has one. I am like a little girl who has got the exact present that she wanted for Christmas.

Most days, I have lunch with Smriti and Mihir in the office cafeteria. But one day, Samir asks me out for lunch, saying we can discuss the very important art tourism project which he plans to introduce in the last quarter of the year.

'Err...,' I hesitate, because somehow, even though I really enjoyed my previous two dates with him, I feel uncomfortable in the office environment, now that he is my boss.

'Do you have other plans? It's okay if you do. I don't mind,' he says.

'No, I just have to tell Smriti and Mihir. They would be waiting,' I say.

'Okay, will meet you at the parking lot then,' he says.

I find them in the cafeteria, and today Leena as well as a few others are with them.

'Hey Nisha, biryani today. It's really good!' says Mihir, as he scoops a spoonful into his mouth. It does look tasty.

'Guys, I am going out for lunch. I won't be joining you today,' I say.

'Ooooh! Someone is going on a date! Who with? Tell, tell!' chimes Smriti.

'It is not a date! I am going out with Samir. It's a working lunch, and I did know him before I started working here,' I defend myself.

I see Leena smirking, but I ignore her and walk out.

As usual, Samir has chosen a magnificent place, one that makes you forget everything the moment you walk in, a place where the ambience relaxes you so much and transports you to a different world. The last thing I want to do is talk about work here. I want to kick off my footwear, sit back with a glass of champagne, and just relax.

But I am on high alert, as I am now Ms Efficiency personified. I remember my disaster on the first date when I had drunk too much, and I definitely have learnt my lesson. I surely do not want to repeat that and spoil the good impression I have now made professionally.

So I opt for a mocktail instead much to the amusement of Samir. We converse mostly about business. Once we get into the discussion, we become so engrossed in it that I forget all about my surroundings. We talk about his pet project—introducing art tourism in India. It is the hottest thing in Europe and major parts of America. There is a conference on art tourism in Bali in a fortnight. Samir and I had been working hard on preparing all the slides for the presentation that he would give, portraying the hotspots in India, and why India could be a great destination for it.

'Nisha, I think you should you accompany me to the Bali conference,' says Samir, taking me totally by surprise.

'Me?' I am taken aback.

'Yes. You will indeed be a valuable resource. Besides, you will also get to learn so much. All the potential investors will be there. You can meet all of them. We need to really make a good impression, Nisha. You have indeed worked hard on it, and besides, you know all the details as much as I do.'

I don't know what to say. This is going to be my first trip abroad ever. Finally my dream of going abroad and having that stamp on my passport can come true! I am elated, overjoyed, and really dancing. I am also secretly thanking my lucky stars that I got a passport made at Akash's insistence while I was still working at Point to Point. I make a mental note to call him up later and thank him. Outside however, I appear calm.

'I hope your dad has no objections to your travel?' asks Samir.

'Naah, I don't think that will be much of a problem,' I say, trying to sound casual.

My father is passive and shows absolutely no reaction, as I dance all the way home and tell him about my trip to Bali. But even his I-don't-give-a-damn attitude cannot dampen my spirit. I volunteer all the details about the conference and how we have been working hard on it and what it means to me. I rattle on endlessly in excitement. I must have never spoken this much to him my entire life. But this is a foreign trip, the first in the family, and it's no small feat.

'Where will you be staying?' he finally asks.

I already know the resort and it is a five-star one. It is out of the world, and the fact that I will soon be there is really a dream come true. I tell him that the company would make arrangements for all that.

I decide to go clothes shopping over the weekend. I no longer need Chetana's help or advice now. Also, I have a lot more money now than I did earlier.

I also call up Akash and thank him for making me apply for the passport. He truly seems overjoyed for me. He says Parinita chucking me out of Point to Point was the best favour she could have ever done to me. Now it may seem so, but while it was happening, I remember how dejected I was. Things truly have a way of turning around. A month back I was desperate, begging for a job, and going for countless interviews. Today I am planning a trip abroad, and my self-esteem has multiplied by leaps and bounds.

No sooner than I hang up after speaking to Akash, the phone rings again. This time it is Prashant. I am surprised as he has never ever called me before. I ask him how he is and he comes straight to the point.

'I heard you are going on a trip abroad with Samir?' he says. His tone is rancid, accusing. I am taken aback at the bitterness in his voice. It is like he cannot stand anything good happening to me. I was 'Nisha—the underdog' back at Point to Point. Now I am a somebody, and it looks like his ego cannot accept it.

'News travels fast. Who told you? I spoke about it only just now to Akash,' I reply.

'Oh, so it is true?' he asks.

Then I realize that Leena must have told him. And if Leena has told him, then the whole office at Magellan must be gossiping about it.

I am annoyed with him. What cheek does he have to call me up and question me?! He wasn't even nice to me when I was his colleague. It was also partly due to him that I lost my job at Point to Point, though things have turned out for the better. But at that time, none of us knew it. My need to rub it in further and really get my revenge, returns.

I want him to burn with jealousy. I want him to regret the way he has behaved with me all this while. I want to once more gloat in my moment of triumph, and this time, it is a genuine achievement, not just a silly date which I am boasting about. So I tell Prashant about the conference, its importance, and about how I cannot reveal what Samir and I have been working on, as it is top secret.

I tell him about the five-star resort we would be staying at. I tell him I am excited and eager and really looking forward to it.

He listens in pin-drop silence. I am happy to have really given it back to him and rendered him speechless. A kind of slow satisfaction is spreading over me.

Then he says in a quiet tone, 'Of course, what else can you expect when you sleep with the boss? You have cleared your way up, spreading your legs. That is all you were worth, and that is all you will remain,' he says.

His words hit me like a shower of arrows. I am so angry that I cannot think straight. My breath is coming in short gasps. I clutch the phone hard in anger. I am so angry that I can barely speak.

'Fuck you, arsehole', I finally manage to say, but he has already hung up.

Prashant has managed to throw a shovel full of ice and dirty muck on my cherished dream.

I am hurt, upset, and angry—all at the same time. Yet it was me who had implied that I had slept with Samir. But still, there was no need to use the words he did and be mean, nasty, and cruel.

I sit for a long time, thinking about it that night, and even though I know Prashant is being deliberately cruel, I still cannot get his words out of my head, and they sting like hell.

Like a Hurricane

The Bali resort is even more picturesque than the brochures portray. It is at a secluded location on a cliff top at Jimbaran Bay. It is cosseted by seventy-five hectares of superbly landscaped gardens and has a two-kilometre-long private coastline, with miles and miles of white sand. The ocean is a colour which I have never seen before. The moment I set foot on the resort, I go speechless at its beauty and perfection. It even has lavish restaurants facing the ocean. The place seems more like a romantic getaway than a venue for a conference.

Samir seems oblivious to the beauty of the resort as he completes the check in formalities. The other delegates too seem to be arriving, and the reception is soon crowded with people of different nationalities, all waiting to check in. Our rooms are adjacent to each other, and the moment I am inside mine, I keep my luggage in the wardrobe, and run my hands on the ultra-luxurious furnishing of the bed. I throw open the blinds and sharply inhale the magnificent view of the ocean, the beauty of it all, and feel so fortunate at getting a chance to experience such luxury. I have never stayed at a five-star resort before and am enjoying and savouring every moment. I bounce up and down on the bed and smile in joy at my childish act.

Then I explore the room further and examine all the shampoos, the conditioners, moisturizers, and various lotions kept in the loo. When I come out, I notice another door in my room and I am curious as to where it opens out to. Perhaps it is a private terrace?

I unlock it and I scream.

There is a near-naked man standing with his back turned to me, wearing the tightest of briefs, his back muscles rippling, and his well-toned buttocks standing out prominently. The man is as startled as me, and when he turns around, I gasp in horror as the slow realization dawns on me that I am looking at Samir who says, 'What the fuck?'

I retreat in haste and shut the door, and when I recover from the shock, I collapse on my bed, laughing uncontrollably.

Oh, the horror of inadvertently seeing your boss nearly naked! I am so darn embarrassed that I want to dig a hole in the bed, crawl inside, and stay there for eternity. I feel like a prized fool to have barged in on him like that. But the silly hotel should have kept the door locked. How was I to know that the rooms had an interconnected door? It is the first time in my life I have even heard of such a thing as rooms with an interconnected door. I try my best to stop laughing, but I find the situation too ridiculous. I nearly jump out of my skin when there is a knock on the same door. I suppress my giggles and open it.

Samir is fully dressed now and to my relief, he is smiling too.

'Oh, Nisha, I am so sorry. I should have warned you. Most of these hotels have rooms which are interconnected. They give them out in pairs, on request,' he says.

'But why in the world would anyone want it?' I ask naively and as soon as I ask, I realize my stupidity.

'Maybe people want it so they can walk in on unsuspecting others when they are changing clothes,' he smiles and winks.

That sets me off again and I laugh and apologize profusely.

'Don't worry about it. Meet me downstairs in an hour and get all the slides. We have to rock this presentation,' he says.

We rock it just fine. Samir seems to have done his homework thoroughly and his public speaking skills are exemplary. I oddly feel very proud of him, as he wraps up the presentation to a rapturous applause.

The rest of the day goes by in a blur. I can see that art tourism is truly a big thing and everybody is very excited about it. It is the first time I am attending a conference like this, and I carefully make notes about everything that each speaker says for easy reference in the future. I look at some of the people in the audience who seem bored. A few have even dozed off in the back seats! I am surprised how they cannot find such a topic interesting. Then again, maybe they have been to a hundred conferences before and are not newbies like me. Whatever it is, I know I am learning a lot and soak it all in like a sponge.

At night, there is a buffet dinner organized at the venue of the conference, but Samir has instead booked a private table for us by the oceanside. I am glad I am wearing a red dress with a plunging neckline. It perfectly accentuates my curves, making me look toned. I match it with red stilettos and a simple diamond bracelet on my wrist. I have never worn such bold colours before nor such jewellery, but I feel this occasion demands it. I feel a bit like Julia Roberts in *Pretty Woman* after she wears the designer stuff. I am rewarded when I see that Samir has a look of pure admiration on his face when he sees me. He says I look stunning and I thank him. He looks gorgeous himself—dressed in a white shirt tucked into a pair of faded denims. My heart beats faster as I gaze at him, getting increasingly drawn to his handsome face. I find all of this wonderfully romantic, but I have no idea what he feels. Why has he booked us a private table? Is he attracted to me as much as I am to him? I reason out that he has indeed asked me on a date twice, before I started working with Magellan. But I still don't know what his intentions about me are and decide to just enjoy the grand time I am having without reading too much into the situation.

The dinner is in a secluded gazebo and the table is set perfectly, down to the slightest of details. There is a lovely bottle of wine chilling and the candles have been lit for effect. The sound of the ocean waves adds to the whole atmosphere.

'You can have a drink now, Nisha. We are outside office timings now,' smiles Samir as he orders a whisky for himself. His tone definitely sounds flirtatious now, or am I wistfully imagining things because of the whole atmosphere of the place?

'I am scared of tripping over like last time.'

'I'll be there to catch your fall, don't worry. Besides, our rooms have an interconnected door, remember?' he smiles wickedly.

Of course he is flirting now.

'How can I forget? But then, I may be too heavy for you.' I smile back, as I remember how droolworthy he looked nearly naked. The guy does have a cute butt and a well-chiselled body.

'Oh, I am a strong man Nisha. Try me!' he says in a low baritone, making me smile.

As dinner progresses, he keeps refilling my glass of wine and orders another whiskey for himself. Both of us are getting drunk beyond the sane limit—he on his whiskey and me on my wine. Slowly, our conversation turns more intimate.

He starts talking about his previous relationship. 'Her name is Jeena,' he says, 'and she taught me how to live. "Jeena sikhaya" as you say it.' His tone is resigned, slightly bitter, and there is a trace of regret and longing in his voice.

Funnily, I feel a stab of jealousy. But I want to know more.

'Was she the one we saw at the party when you called me a witch for guessing?' I pry.

'Yes, the same.'

'What happened between you two? Why did you split?'

'Let's just say we wanted different things from life. It's a long story, Nisha. One night will not be enough. Let's not talk about it,' he says, and I can see that he is still hurting. I feel angry with Jeena for causing him pain, even though I have never really met her. I am surprised at the intensity of my emotion.

'Tell me about your childhood, Nisha. I want to know,' he says.

The fact that he even bothers to ask, fills me with a kind of tenderness that I find hard to comprehend. My childhood was not a happy one at all. I have never spoken about it to anybody, as I have never had anyone close enough with whom I could share stuff like this. But when he asks, I want to tell him all. I want to tell him how lonely it was growing up without a mother, in the company of a father who didn't seem to care much. I want to tell him how I used to long for some kind of praise when I did exceedingly well in school. I want to tell him that I badly wanted my parents around for all the school events, but my father never came. I want to tell him how it felt to be teased all my life for being plump. How it hurt and how I gradually learnt to shrug it all off with a smile. I want to tell him a lot of things. But I hold back.

'There is nothing to tell,' I say and sigh. 'My mum died when I was five. My dad raised me with the help of a nanny. He hardly speaks to me. I guess I remind him too much of my mother. I am told he loved her a lot,' I add as I clench my fists.

Samir reaches over and holds my hand. Then he raises both my hands and kisses them. My heart nearly stops beating. I realize we have just crossed a line here, and I am not drunk enough to not figure that out. An inner voice inside me screams that it is not a good idea to enter into a relationship with your boss. But the sensation is too good to pass and I am left with an intense longing for more. I want more of it. Nobody has cared this much for me before this.

We walk on the moonlit beach after dinner and it feels so *right*. My heart is thudding in its rib cage, making me feel giddy. I have had way too much wine. He puts his arm around me to steady me and I adore him for it.

We walk in silence on the white sand in the moonlight, the waves splashing at our feet. It is just him and me and miles of white sand lit up by the light of the moon. I notice a few white crabs scuttling away and I laugh in delight.

'Oh Nisha, how easily you laugh! And what tiny things amuse you!' he says gently, looking so tenderly at me, as though seeing me for the first time.

That statement of his does it. All my self-control melts. I want him more than anything else. Who knows, I might never get a chance like this again. We would go back to office and our real lives tomorrow, where I would be back to being Ms Efficiency, making sure his coffee is perfect. Here and now is my moment, where I can be Cinderella.

Do what your heart tells you to. Life is short. Kiss him now.

I look at his hard mouth and his cool eyes, the moonlight highlighting his perfect features. I yank him against me, and the only thing that registers is the surprised look in his eyes as my mouth reaches out to his. He responds with an intensity that takes me aback and his arms go around my waist, pulling me closer to him. He kisses me tenderly, and I feel the heat of his body pumping fire into me. My body trembles and I moan in pleasure.

There is no stopping us now. His hands are caressing my breasts and he has slid them inside my dress. I cannot think straight at all. I am charged with a purely feminine rush, giddy with excitement, as every fibre in my body seems to respond to his touch. We are so hungry for each other. His hands are impatient and there is fire in his blood.

Finally, he pulls away and says hoarsely, 'Let's go back to the room and finish what you started.'

We enter the lift in silence, breathing hard, and we can't wait to get into his room. As soon as we are inside the room, he tugs at my dress and feasts on my breasts. His hands are quick and exploring. There is a trail of my clothes from the door to his bed. In the heat of the moment, I forget to be shy. I want him as badly as he wants me.

He is on top of me, him panting and me moaning in delight. I am oblivious to any other sensation as he plunges into me and I arch back, acceding to his urgent demands. He drives into me and something inside me explodes. It is like a turbulent wave that has seared my very soul. He takes me higher and I call out his name in pure pleasure. And finally he melts and lies down beside me, running his hands through my hair. I am crying in joy, the kind of which I have never felt before.

He kisses me again, and this time gently on my mouth. I love him so very much at that moment, that if he had asked me to cut out my heart and give it to him, I would gladly have done it. He is tracing my nose with his fingers now, and all I can do is shyly tug the sheet and cover my nakedness. Now that it is over, I want to be covered, as I am aware my body is far from perfect, whereas he is like Adonis.

'You are gorgeous,' he says, his fingers still tracing my features. He is lying on his side, with one arm supporting his head.

'It was my first time,' I say softly.

'Oh, Nisha! I am so darn sorry. I would have been gentler had I known any better.'

Oh, if he only knew how happy he has made me! Nobody has ever made me feel the way he has. I feel whole and complete. I feel satisfied. I feel content. I have never known such joy, such serenity before this. He makes me feel like I am truly gorgeous. He makes me feel *loved*, something that I haven't felt in a long, long time.

'You are perfect, Samir,' I say, and I mean it completely.

And at that moment, I know that it is truly what I believe with my entire heart and soul.

Slave to Love

The next morning, we do it all over again before the break of dawn. And this time too it is as urgent, as demanding as the previous night. Like a broken dam whose flood of water submerges the both of us, the force is too powerful to resist. When we finish, I scramble hurriedly for the covers, wrapping the bed sheet around me protectively, much to Samir's amusement.

'Hurry, or we will get late for the first session today,' I call out, as I go back to my room through the interconnected door.

'Relax Nisha, we can afford to miss the first session. Come back here right now!' he says with affection.

'No! I do want to listen to the head of Cruise Line Corporation speak. I have only read about him in magazines. This is a real opportunity for me.'

'That's what I like about you, Nisha. You do grab every single opportunity, don't you?'

'Get out of bed right now and get ready. And please stop staring at me!'

'Yes boss,' he says and laughs heartily.

It is only when I am by myself, I realize what Chetana meant all those months ago, when she said 'You never know,' while helping me with the dress for my date with Prashant. I rummage through my bag and her morning-after pills are still there. I thank her silently as I pop one into my mouth.

Later, as we walk towards the conference room, I feel really awkward. It's like I am carrying a large banner which reads, 'I had awesome sex last night and this morning too.' Of course, no one can tell, but I still feel very awkward, as though they can guess for themselves.

I push my emotions aside and try hard to not stare at Samir. The presentation scheduled for the day is really interesting and time soon flies. I make notes and catch Samir smiling at me. I smile back and then do my best to ignore him. By the end of the day, we just can't wait to be with each other again. As soon as the programme for the day is over, we rush into the hotel room.

I do not know if it is plain lust or the ambience of this place that is making me desire him so much. Is it because 'Nisha-the-plain-Jane' has bagged herself an Adonis?

Hold on, you haven't bagged him. You have only had casual sex and there is a difference, you know. He hasn't made any promises, nor has he even indicated or implied that it is anything more than sex.

Go away. Let me have my Cinderella moments in peace. You know I deserve it.

And when we are alone by ourselves, he does make me feel like a princess. He treats me like I am the only woman on earth. Nobody has treated me with such reverence before. He kisses my toes and then sucks on them. I gasp in pleasure. He touches all of me gently, light butterfly strokes, and makes me literally beg for more. Later, he holds me close and says he is going to make me very happy soon. He already has. We stay in bed that night and order dinner in. I stare at the bedside clock, wishing for time to come to a standstill. I do not want these moments to end. I don't want to go back to Mumbai. I wish we could stay in this cocooned space of our own forever. It is so darn comforting, and I feel so content in his arms.

Our flight is only for the next evening. There is a cycling tour organized in the morning for all the visiting delegates. The brochure, which came along with the programme schedule for the day, says that one can cycle into the traditional Balinese village, explore the carved temples set amidst breathtaking natural beauty, and stop for a sip of tender coconut water while chatting with farmers and wood carvers. The route is along a mountain trail and is an insight into the lives of the local farmers, away from the tame package tourism that most resorts offer.

'Would you like to go?' asks Samir.

First, there is a confession I have to make,' I say. 'I cannot ride a bicycle.'

'What? You cannot ride a bicycle?' He sounds genuinely surprised.

'Most people learn bicycle riding in childhood, but the thing is that I had no one to teach me as a child,' I say.

It brings back painful memories of when I would watch the children in my apartment go riding on their bicycles. I would watch longingly and get teased with taunts like, 'Ugly fatso can't ride a bike' or 'Big pig can't ride a bike.' I wanted to ride a bicycle like them more than anything else in the world. I even asked my father if he would get me one, to which he replied, 'A bicycle? What for?', and that had been the end of the conversation. I had been dismissed. I remember the years of loneliness, the years of pain, and it all comes back to haunt me like it happened yesterday. How can one feel *so alone and so helpless*? Funny how it still has the power to hurt *this much,* even when one is a full-grown adult.

'Oh Nisha, there are better things to do in life than go on a silly bike ride,' says Samir. He walks over to me and hugs me.

'You know, your eyes are so expressive. They reflect what you feel immediately. I hate the look of sadness in them. Wipe them away,' he says and kisses me tenderly on my forehead.

I promptly burst into tears, startling him with my action. I have no idea why. Maybe it is because I had thought that this was just about sex for him, and had not in the least expected him to *care* about me. Tenderness is something I have never had in my life, and receiving it so suddenly has totally taken me by surprise.

The Bali trip has indeed been a crossover point in my relationship with him. At that moment, I am too overwhelmed, too excited, and it is all too new to even analyse and consider where it is heading.

When we get back to office, it is really hard to hide my feeling for him from others.

Smriti asks me, 'So how was your first trip abroad? As exciting as you thought?'

Even more exciting than I could ever possibly imagine. You have no idea!

'Yeah, it was okay. I did learn a lot. Made a lot of notes.'

'Well, good for you, girl!' she says, and gets back to work.

I sigh with relief. Had she asked me a few more questions, she would have probably started to notice how uncomfortable I was discussing the Bali trip.

Later, it occurs to me that when Samir and I had absolutely nothing between us, I wanted to boast and imply there was something more. But now that there is indeed something more (whether it is lust or love, I really cannot tell at this point), I want to hide it, tuck away my little secret, hug it close to my heart, and not share it with anybody.

I try to be as professional at work as possible. Samir is a really busy man, and I throw myself full throttle into my work. But now, on most days, he wants me to have lunch with him and when he does ask, I can hardly refuse. We spend a lot of time together. A lot more than is strictly necessary, really.

Samir has another trip scheduled to Hyderabad for a branch appraisal visit and he wants me to accompany him for that as well. It is a two-day trip. At work, we conduct ourselves in a very professional manner. We meet the branch manager and discuss business plans, strategies, and the issues which need focussing. The Hyderabad branch is lacking in some areas, and Samir gives some really good suggestions as to what they can do. He tells me to draw up a detailed plan of action. I give my inputs and the branch manager gives his. It is a fruitful meeting, and Samir is happy with the outcome and the systems which have been put in place.

Of course, we have dinner together in the hotel room straight after the meetings, and of course we have sex. Really good 'can't-wait-to-get-my-hands-on-you' sex. What I find amazing is that he is as hungry for me as I am for him. It is as good as the time we had in Bali. Prashant's taunting words come back to haunt me at times. But I push them aside because this is something so powerful and so addictive, almost like a drug. I am old enough to know my own mind, and I know I want to be with him, more than anything else in the world. Also, there is no one to whom I can speak about it, although once or twice after sex, I am indeed tempted to tell Samir about what Prashant had said. But the moments are too tender and too passionate to spoil with such off-putting talk, and talking about what he said would be like throwing a bag of rotten garbage in a beautiful, calm sanctorum. So I push aside his hurtful words and carry on.

Soon, we are having lunch together on all days. We also work together late into the night and leave together on most days, with Samir insisting on dropping me home. I vehemently protest and decline to accept. After much persuasion, he gives in to my protests, insisting on dropping me at least to the train station every day.

We cannot hide our affair for long. Nobody has spoken to me directly about it so far, but I know that the entire office is talking about it. I can hear their hushed whispers at the coffee-vending machine and how they all go very quiet as soon as they spot me.

I can see the smirk on Leena's face whenever I go into Samir's cabin to discuss something. I know Smriti is dying to ask me about it, but is holding her silence. I don't feel very happy about it, but now Samir has become my daily fix, something that I cannot seem to get enough of. I want to see him every day, I want to talk to him, be there for him, be a part of every single thing he does.

But the whole office talking about it is bothering me too. Prashant's words fester inside me like a dormant volcano waiting to explode. While on the one hand I feel elated, thrilled, and overjoyed to be this involved in Samir's life, on the other hand, I somehow feel uncomfortable and uneasy. It is strange to have these conflicting emotions.

It has been five months since the Bali trip. Of course I am sleeping with the boss. But it is not like what Prashant implies. I am also very good at my work. Over the last couple of months, ever since the Bali and the Hyderabad trips, I have realized that I am indeed in love with him. I also know that I have never ever loved anyone or given myself to anyone the way I have given myself so totally to him. All my earlier one-sided crushes seem to pale in comparison to what I feel for him. I know this is the real deal. I am dependent on him. I have given away my heart to him, and he has total control over it. He can crush it, throw it away, toss it aside. Or he can value it. I have given the power of my very life to him. I truly and completely *need* him now. It is a very scary feeling.

And there is not a single soul on this planet with whom I can talk about this. Once or twice, I do consider calling up Chetana or even Akash. But somehow I have travelled so far down this road that I would have a lot of explaining to do. So I do not call them and continue with my intoxicated state of being this involved with him. I am also now on the pill, having regular sex, and really enjoying my life.

Yet one part of me feels like I am on a roller coaster travelling at top speed, and there is no way to stop it or get off.

I am trapped, it is my own doing, and I do not know what to do. And the surprising this is that I don't even know if I want to get off anymore.

Sound of Silence

At work, Samir is the perfect boss. Outside work, he is the perfect boyfriend. It is strange how easily we are able to switch between the two modes. Sleeping with someone for five months surely qualifies him as boyfriend, doesn't it? Twice, I have even slept over at his place, when we have had to work very late. Like he said, it made no sense to go all the way home by train, when I had to rush back to work the very next morning.

Both the times that I stayed over, I simply slept in his bedroom and not the guest room. The last time I was there, I had gone over to the guest bedroom, opened the drawer, and looked for the earrings. But they were gone.

I say nothing about it for nearly two weeks.

When I cannot hold it inside me anymore, I decide to ask him about it. The opportunity to do so comes the very next day, while having lunch at a small bistro near the office.

'Oh! How in the world did you even know about those earrings? You really are a witch!' he says. He sounds surprised that I brought it up.

‘Remember when I hurt my leg and stayed over? I had found them then, but did not know you well enough to ask you about it.’

‘And you think you know me well now?’ he asks amusedly, eyes twinkling

‘I know you well in bed at least, Mr Sharma. I know your appointments and what you do and where you go and who you meet. I even know what kind of underwear you prefer. Now stop changing the topic and tell me about the earrings.’

‘They are Jeena’s. She called and asked for them. Apparently they are her favourite pair.’

‘You never told me.’ It comes out accusingly. If jealousy is a hand grenade, he has just bitten the plug. I am ready to explode with it. And God, it hurts too. How could he not tell me that he had met her?

‘There was nothing to tell. It is a closed chapter, Nisha. It is over. I have moved on.’

But I am not satisfied and want to know more.

‘So where did you meet her? Did she come to your place?’ I prod.

‘Eh? Hell no! I did not want to see her. She is the one who called me and told me to look for them in the first place. I found them, put them in an envelope, and gave it to the receptionist, from whom she collected them herself.’

I feel so relieved and so stupidly happy to hear this. A slow grin spreads over my face. Then I lean across over the table and kiss him on his cheek, right where his dimple appears when he smiles. I adore him for the fact that he chose not to meet Jeena.

'I absolutely and totally love you Samir,' I say, surprising myself. It is the very first time I have confessed it to him.

'Oh Nisha, I love you too,' he says somewhat abashedly. And he smiles. I could have been knocked over with a feather that moment.

I want to cuddle him, hold him in my arms, and never let him go. He is almost shy. It is the first time I see this side of Samir. He looks so boyish and so vulnerable, not like the successful, savvy businessman that he is. My heart turns into squashed pulp looking at his shy smile and the dimple on his cheek. His face is radiating happiness. I want to kiss him again, but we have already created a small scene when I stood up and leaned over to kiss him. This is a quiet place and the regulars at the bistro, mostly the retired older folks, had turned to look when they heard me pushing back my chair. We must have shocked them with our PDA.

It is a month later at a very exotic resort in Kerala where Samir finally pops the question. We have finished a two-day conference at Kochi, and Samir and I have both taken a day off. We have driven from Kochi to this amazing place called Munnar. Nestled among tea plantations is a lovely private bungalow which Samir has rented for our stay. It is a scene straight out of a movie, and all I can do is gasp in pleasure as we drive to the destination. When the bungalow finally comes into view, with mist all around, the cold mountain air, the tall, deciduous trees— it seems almost straight out of a picture postcard scene.

We check into our room and I am delighted with the quaint way in which it has been done up, with antique furniture all around. We make love and he chooses the apt moment to ask.

'Nisha, my one and only love, will you be my wife?' he says.

I laugh in delight.

'What took you so long to ask?' I reply.

'Well, I had to see how good you were in bed first, and it took me this long to assess you. I am marrying you only for the sex, you know,' he says with a straight face. I pommel his head with a pillow and he quickly ducks under another pillow and roars with laughter.

At that moment, I know that I mean the world to him. I know he truly loves me. I know he needs me as much as I need him. I cannot believe how lucky I have been. What a turn my life has taken. Who would have thought that it would change so drastically in five months time, when I first accepted the job offer at Magellan? My cup of joy is overflowing, and I want to stand in the mountains and shout out to the world that I am getting married to the person who means the world to me.

'By the way, my family doesn't know it yet,' he says.

'Would your mother not want you to have an arranged marriage with a slim, rich girl who matches your family background?' I ask.

We have hardly talked about his mother or brother in these five months and I had almost forgotten they exist. This is the first time I feel somewhat inadequate with my lower-middle-class upbringing. He has been born with a silver spoon in his mouth and I seem to have clawed my way into his heart. He is classy and I am down to earth. He is sophisticated and I am simple. He knows his wines and cutlery while I prefer to eat with my hands. He knows his caviar from his cheese. To me, they all taste like rubber, which would probably sound like blasphemy in the social circles he moves in. I imagine a scene where his mother accuses me of trapping her son. And then banishes him from her inheritance because he has chosen to marry beneath his status. I imagine his relatives sadly shaking their heads and saying that Samir must be off his senses to have found this plain, lower-middle-class plump girl suitable to be his wife, while he could have had the pick of women.

'Hey, no Nisha! This is where you are mistaken. My mother and brother are really cool. They will be perfectly okay with whatever I choose to do. But I will definitely have to speak to your dad.' he says.

'I am not really close to my dad Samir. You know how it is,' I say.

'Yeah I know, but the right thing for me to do is speak to him. Tell me when I can come to your place and meet him.'

I tell him that I will break the news to my father first, and then set up a meeting with him over the weekend.

My father is watching television when I decide to break the news to him.

'Papa, there is something I have to tell you,' I say, waiting for him to acknowledge me.

He takes a sip of the buttermilk that he always drinks after his meal and continues watching television.

I clear my throat and wait for him to respond.

He is perhaps hoping that I will vanish like I usually do. But today, I do no such thing. I instead wait patiently, dreaming of Samir.

My mobile buzzes just then and it is a text from Samir.

'Have you spoken to him?' it reads.

'Not yet, in the process.' I text back.

'Do it soon and call me,' comes the quick reply.

'Papa,' I say again, and this time he grunts.

I tell him that I have been working closely with my boss for the last five months. I tell him that he is one of the major shareholders in Magellan International. I talk about his educational qualifications and how he is as a person. Then I tell him that he has asked me to marry him and he wants to come and meet my father.

There is absolutely no reaction from my father. He is like stone, sitting there totally impassive, and continuing to sip his buttermilk. I am so angry, I want to knock it over. I want him to say something. I want him to be happy for me. Or express anger. Or any damn expression. Not just sit there like a wall, which is what he has been doing all these past years. What about me? What have I done? Is it my fault that my mother died? I wish and wish my mother was around. At least she would have shared my joy. My dad still continues sitting there.

Finally I ask, 'Papa, don't you have anything to say?'

'What is the guy's name?' he asks with great effort, as though saying those words have placed an immense strain on his brain.

'His name is Samir, Papa,' I answer dutifully. 'He wants to meet you,' I add.

I think even if I told him that the Prime Minister of India was asking for my hand in marriage, it would not have made an iota of difference to him. I am angry now at Samir for insisting that I tell my father. But then, what choice was I left with? Should I have eloped and got married instead? A little voice inside my head screams that even that would not really made a difference to him.

'Okay, we will meet,' he says finally.

'When, Papa? Can I tell him to come this Saturday at four in the evening?' I ask.

'Okay,' he says, as he goes back to sipping his buttermilk and watching television, and I know I have been dismissed.

I barge into my room angrily and call Samir to tell him all that has happened. Samir asks me to keep my cool and be patient. We talk for long about the wedding plans amongst other things. He says that he wants to have a really simple ceremony, maybe an Arya Samaj one, with very limited people. I truly do not have anyone to call. I am not in touch with any of my relatives on my mother's side, and my dad is a single child himself, having lost his mother when he was five or so. He was raised by his aunt who has passed away, and I don't think my dad too will have anyone to invite. So I am just happy to go along with anything that Samir suggests.

There are just two days left for Saturday, when Samir will meet my dad. Somehow I am nervous about the meeting. Samir has never come to my home before and the truth is, I am somewhat ashamed of my modest little home. The next two days pass off immersed in work, and as soon as I reach home, I try my best to make the home look a little more presentable.

On Saturday morning, I wake up early and glance at the clock. It is 7.30 a.m. My routine on weekends is to sleep late, but that day I cannot sleep. On weekdays, no matter how early I wake up, I usually find my dad sitting on the balcony, in his easy chair, sipping his tea while reading the paper. But on that particular morning he is missing.

I check the loo and find he isn't there either. Puzzled, I look in his room and to my surprise, he is still asleep. I wait for an hour more. Then I decide to wake him up with tea. I make tea and walk to his room and keep it beside his bed.

'Papa, wake up. It's time for your morning cup of tea,' I say.

There is no response from him and I repeat myself again. When he again does not respond, my heart starts beating rapidly and I touch his forehead. It is icy cold. I try to feel his breath but I feel nothing, giving rise to my worst fears. I am so afraid that he is dead. I stand there like a dumb fool, not knowing what to do.

I am petrified. Then with shaking hands, I dial Samir's number. 'Why is he taking so long to answer the phone?' I mutter with increasing worry.

Finally when he does, groggy with sleep, I break down and tell him that I think my father is dead.

He tells me he will be right over, and keeping true to his word, he is at my home in twenty minutes. I have been pacing up and down the room the whole time, not knowing what to do, and I keep going to the balcony and peering to see if I can spot his car. He has called for an ambulance too and arrives minutes before the ambulance does.

The paramedics shift my father on to a stretcher and we follow the ambulance in his car. We rush to emergency and the duty doctor checks for his pulse and then examines him with a stethoscope. Then shaking his head, the doctor says, 'I am sorry, but I cannot get a pulse. He is dead. Nurse, note it down as a case of dead on arrival.'

It Must Have Been Love

Present day

Mumbai

Thoughts are whirling madly around me. My head is in utter turmoil. On the one hand I am angry. How in the world can Samir just phone me and tell me our marriage is over? What the hell? On the other hand, the reality that he *can* do so and has indeed *done* so, sinks in slowly like the gradual drizzle of rain. It is only when the water is ankle deep that I realize it had been building up slowly all along and that something has to be done about it now. And Samir has done it.

The pain of it is too much to bear. It feels like a million pieces of shrapnel have entered my heart. It becomes increasingly unbearable. Were all these years a mere joke for him?

With trembling fingers, I dial his number. He does not answer. My heart sinks. I dial again.

This time he picks up.

'Samir' I say. My voice is a hoarse whisper. I am unable to stand upright, sitting on the floor on our balcony, my head bent low, and the phone cradled in one ear. I am so emotional, I can barely speak.

'Look Nisha, the writing has been on the wall for a few years now. Don't pretend you did not notice it. I am sorry it has to come to this, but it is over,' he says ever so calmly and so very clearly. There is not a trace of emotion in his voice. It is the calm, collected, and unaffected way that he says it which does me in. How can he? How is he so cold, so heartless? Can't he hear the plea in my voice begging him to come back? There is a huge lump in my throat and I start breathing rapidly. When I try to speak, no words come out. I am speechless.

Tears cloud my eyes. What writing? What wall? Why is he doing this? It makes no sense to me.

My hands start shaking again, and the intensity of the pain is too much to bear. I am unable to talk at all. He cuts the call abruptly. I feel as though someone has held my head and smashed it hard against a rock. I feel as though I will explode.

Did the past eight years mean nothing to him? Do his children mean nothing to him? Granted, it was me who was very keen to have them, even though he did not want children just then. But then, I have totally kept up my end of the bargain. I have been with them, day in and day out, with him doing only a guest appearance in their lives. It is me who chose Tanya's school, it is me who held her though the sleepless nights, it is me who changed her diapers and took her for her vaccinations, it is me who was there for every parent–teacher meeting, for every single time she performed on stage. I was there through and through. I want to scream at him. I want to tear out his hair. I want to claw him and demand justice.

The phone beeps and it is a text from him.

'Please do not try to call me. I am moving in with Maya. Will contact you over the next couple of days and will try and sort out things.'

That really kills me. It is the final stab, cold and brutal. There I have it. In black and white. He has left me for a younger woman. A bloody good-looking slimmer, smarter woman.

I run to his cupboard and to my utter shock, I see that almost all his clothes are gone. How could I have not known? When did he pack? Was I so engrossed in Tanya and Rohit that I had not even noticed? Some of his other clothes remain neatly stacked in the cupboard. His belts and ties are there. It is too painful to look at them, and I shut his wardrobe with a pounding heart.

My heart now feels like a stone. I burst into tears and I cry. I cry for all that has happened. I cry for Tanya and baby Rohit. I cry for all the years that I have spent with him which now feel like a sham. I cry for the fool I have been. But mostly, I feel terribly sorry for that stupid silly Nisha who thought that she had found heaven, the day that she married Samir and moved into his home.

How naive and foolish one is at twenty-six. How things change! Who would have thought it would come to this?

I cry for hours. The sound is alien to my own ears as it is a wounded cry I never thought I was capable of emitting, and finally, when I have exhausted my tears, I go into the children's room. Little Tanya is sleeping peacefully in her bed, blissfully unaware that her mother's world has just shattered into a million pieces.

She sleeps peacefully on the pink princess bed, with its motif of a crown and the other embellishments she chose herself on her sixth birthday.

'I am a big girl now, Mama, and I will sleep on my own,' she had said.

Baby Rohit is in a crib next to her, the same crib which Tanya had used as an infant. I kiss Tanya tenderly, taking in the softness of the cheek and the sheer innocence of her face. For a moment, I marvel at how blissful a child's sleep can be. She does not even stir in her sleep. I kiss Rohit and inhale the warm baby smell, a mixture of talcum powder and softness, and that special love which babies seem to radiate.

This brings a fresh set of tears, but I bite them back quickly.

Finally, I sit on the floor next to Tanya, and no sooner do I rest my head on her bed, I fall asleep exhausted.

She wakes me up the next morning and I am unable to open my eyes.

'Silly Mama! You slept on the floor. Wake up. Have you been drinking wine, Mama?' she says, admonishing me in that tone she adopts when she feels she is right. She is precocious for a seven-year-old. I have always felt that she is an old soul in a young body.

I am up with a start, hearing her voice. It takes me a few seconds to figure out why I am there, and then all the events of the previous night come rushing back in. I feel like somebody has punched me hard in the face. But I have to put up a calm face for Tanya.

'What nonsense you talk. You know Mama never

drinks when papa isn't home,' I say and I wince inside, for I know what she will ask next.

Sure enough, she asks, 'Mama, where is Papa?'

'He is travelling. He has gone to Germany and will not be back for a while,' I say. I have no idea from where Germany has come up. I hurriedly help Tanya get ready for school, by which time Rohit wakes up too.

Taking care of Rohit is not much of a challenge (although a little time-consuming), as his is a pretty set routine consisting of the usual sleep-eat-bathe-play-sleep pattern. He is a real darling and is no trouble to look after at all, unlike Tanya who was a cranky, fussy, colicky baby as an infant.

I am able to get through most of the morning because Rohit needs my constant attention. Finally when he sleeps, I get some time to myself, as there are still a couple of hours left before Tanya comes back from school.

I still cannot believe Samir has left me. Is this all a dream? I go to my phone and read his text again. A fresh wave of pain floods me. I look at our couple picture on the mantelpiece clicked during our honeymoon in Seychelles eight years back. The picture shows a younger and slimmer version of me. He still looks as gorgeous as he did on the day we got married. He has never missed his gym routine and still has a body that most men only dream of having.

Which Maya must now be discovering. I feel sick and nauseous at the very thought. She means more to him now than me. I have been discarded, thrown out. I have lived my 'use-by date'.

In the photograph, his arms are around me, hugging me lovingly from behind. We are looking into the camera and smiling the smile of newlyweds, oblivious to the world around them, who need nobody but each other. Where, or when, did it all start going wrong? Why has he taken this drastic step of walking out?

I think back about all our years together. He did change a little after his mother's death and was not his usual self and for a while had stopped communicating with me. But then, I had presumed that it was the normal depression that everyone goes through when they lose a parent. When had he changed this much? *How had I been so darn oblivious to it?*

Then I remember the journals which I started writing after my father passed away.

I am gripped with an overwhelming urge to read them now. They are in a suitcase, stored in the loft above the study. I drag the aluminium ladder towards the loft, climbing up to reach the dusty suitcase which contains all the journals, my college magazines, and some old, sentimental stuff which I did not have the heart to throw away. There are also at least eighty cards in there which Samir had given me in the early years of our marriage. How then can love die? Isn't marriage supposed to be a 'happily ever after'?

I find my journal and begin to read.

Nisha's journals

2001

August 18th

Friday

How many people in the world get married within a month of their father's death, and then go straight for a honeymoon in Seychelles? Not many, I would guess. Put like that it sounds cold, I know. But then, I really was left with no other choice. It made no sense to live in that apartment alone by myself.

Samir is a sweetheart. I could have never coped with all the funeral arrangements without him. He even lit the funeral pyre, something reserved for only a son. I don't even remember the faces of the handful of people who turned up for the funeral. My father was a recluse, a lonely man who kept mostly to himself. I think the only people who really came were the people from my building, some of whom I knew. I did feel sorry for him. He lived his whole life with a closed heart ever since my mother died. In all the years that I have known him, I do not remember any person ever visiting us as his friend. He had lived his life in pain and punishment, but he had inflicted it on himself and, in a less obvious way, on me too, by shutting me out completely from his life. I had *learnt to suppress my pain and disguise it with a big smile and my wit. How I had longed for his approval all my life. How I had longed for him to just once appreciate my school marks. My heart had cried and cried all through the growing up years. I had tried and tried to get through to him, but he had always remained a stone. The tears had all dried up now. In a strange way, I felt like a huge burden was lifted off me. I did not shed a single tear at his passing away.*

I guess a part of me should have been grateful to him for bringing me up. Had he been a loving father who genuinely cared, who had been there for me when I needed him most, maybe I would have felt grateful. But I am not grateful at all. It does feel a bit odd to refer to him in past tense, but that is about all I feel, to be honest.

I don't think anyone will ever understand me unless they have lived my life. Not even Samir. So I prefer expressing it here. If I do not express it, I sometimes feel I will explode. Writing here feels cathartic, and I am glad I started a journal. It helps me cope.

2001
August 30th
Wednesday

How strange it is that destiny or the universe or whatever force it is, has a way of making things fall into place perfectly. When Samir had suggested the Arya Samaj wedding and a simple, no-frills ceremony, I had not even thought in detail about it and had agreed. But now in retrospect, it has fitted perfectly with the society's conception of the 'proper thing to do'. I can play the grief-stricken bride.

All of Samir's relatives are present. His mother and brother have flown in from London especially for the wedding. So have some of his other folks from around the globe. If they found it too odd that only Chetana and Akash are a part of it from my side, they were too sophisticated, polite, and considerate to comment on it. But what can I do? Chetana and Akash are the closest people I have had, really. I never had any real friends in school or college. I know most people would find my existence to be a lonely one, but I was fine, really!

I am glad that his mother is going back tomorrow. His

brother left just after the wedding. His mother stayed around till we got back from our honeymoon.

(Oh, it was bliss! Seychelles is pure heaven on earth! I particularly enjoyed the lovemaking sessions under the canopy of stars on our very private deck. And my treasured memory is how we skinny-dipped, and how Samir had laughed in shock and delight! Oh, I adore him with all my heart and am so, so, so happy I found him. He truly makes me feel like I am the luckiest woman on earth!)

His mother is nice and non-interfering. But somehow, I cannot connect much with her. Maybe secretly she disapproves of me—I don't know. Samir says it is all in my head. But I do have to wear a salwar-kameez when she is around. (How could I refuse Samir when he asked so sweetly between kisses whether I would wear a salwar-kameez when his mother was around?) I would have thought that staying in London she would be a little more Westernized, but she seems to have regressed into being more Indian. Anyway, it's just until tomorrow, and then she goes back.

Samir resumes work tomorrow. I sure am going to feel strange being all by myself in this huge apartment. Samir somehow felt my continuing to work in office would not be good for his image. How can his wife be his secretary?!

I did not like how he implied that a secretary's job was something menial. But I did not want to argue with him. I guess he does have a point after all.
It remains to see how I will pass my time. Maybe I will learn to cook and read!

With a Little Help From My Friends

Reading the journal has brought back a flood of memories. It is as though a door which had been closed has suddenly opened, and you have discovered an entirely new room in your home which you had forgotten existed. It is like I want to retrace every single thing that happened ever since Samir and I got married, to examine and see if there were signs or warnings of something amiss in our marriage all along. Till Samir walked out, I never knew what pain *really* feels like. Never had I felt like this—not even when my father died. This pain—it feels like a vicious beast attacking me, baring its menacing claws and teeth when I am bound and gagged, and it will get my throat any moment now. Mostly, I feel helpless.

There is nothing I can do. And I think it is mostly my outrage at the injustice of it all that is making me want to wail out loudly. Tears stream down my cheeks and I get up to wash my face. Then I make a cup of tea for myself. And I settle down on the rocking chair in the balcony with my journals again.

It is funny how eight years change you, make you forget the tiny details. But when you open that door, it suddenly comes back crystal clear. It is as though the journal is the key to my past. It is as though by looking back, I can make some sense of the pieces that my life now lies in.

The next entry in the journal is on November 11, 2001.

It is just a very short entry which reads:

There are certain things that change after marriage, things which nobody will understand till they get married. Non-issues suddenly become issues. Now your spouse has a say in who your friends can be and who should remain strictly off limits. Your spouse can now also pass judgements about people whom they know little about, but most of all people who have been longer in your life than they have. I think it is very unfair.

Chetana and Akash came home today.

I wish now they had not.

The entry ends abruptly there, and I think back and recall that day in vivid detail.

It had been three weeks since I joined the baking and cooking course. I had told Samir that I was beginning to get bored at home after ten days of staying put, and that I was contemplating joining some cooking course.

'You are going to cook?' he had asked smiling.

'Come on! I am not that bad a cook. Haan, I might not be as good as your Baiju Maharaj yet, but wait and see. You will soon be begging for stuff I cook.'

'You know, Nisha, how diet-conscious I am. I am careful about what I eat, and Baiju knows exactly what I want. He's been with me for ages. Just leave the cooking to him.'

I did feel a bit upset at the way he put it so frankly. But a marriage is all about honesty, isn't it? I do know how very careful he is about his diet, and how he will not miss his workout at the gym for anything in the world (A lean, taut, muscular body like that of Adonis does not come without all that hard work). But still, there was no need to be so upfront about it.

'Okay, Samir. I won't do the course and I won't cook for you. Happy?'

'Hey, Nisha. Don't get upset. Go do the course! It makes you happy, right?'

'It's not that it makes me happy, Samir. You are at work the whole day and when you come back, you don't want to talk about it. I am at home the whole day. Cooking and cleaning is taken care of by your efficient staff.'

'Not "your", my love, it is now "OUR". This home is as much yours as it is mine,' he gently corrects me.

'Well, what I am saying is that this is not how it used to be before, Samir. I felt good at work, I felt good discussing every project with you, and how you valued my inputs. And now suddenly I am at home, with nothing to do except waiting for you to get back. Then you don't even want to discuss things that happened at office with me anymore.'

'I leave my office worries in the office itself, Nisha. And besides, when have we really talked work after office? I need to unwind once I get back home, I need to take a breather, and talking about work is a strain. I thought you of all people would understand that.'

He was right as usual, of course. In office, we gave work our hundred per cent, but once we left office, we made it a point not to talk about it. We just ended up having some amazing sex and we were recharged for the next day.

'Yeah, Samir, you're right. I don't know why I am getting so worked up these days.'

He had kissed me on the forehead and said, 'Go do the course baby, you will feel good.'

The course turns out to be a very good one. When it came to cooking, I knew only the basic items like rice, dal, rotis, and a few vegetables. In my growing up years, Malati Tayi had cooked for us, and after she passed away, I had managed the basics. My father never cooked, except for the regular cups of tea he made for himself. He had once said that my mother had been a really superb cook. So maybe it was genetic, I don't know, but I find myself really interested in learning all that the course instructor has to teach. She is Mrs Indrayani, a round, fat, Punjabi lady, and she proudly announces that food is her passion. It shows.

We have learnt how to bake a mouth-watering pineapple cake. The course includes everything—right from starters to main course to desserts. It includes the basic dishes from four styles, namely, Mughlai, Continental, Indian, and Chinese. I get to learn the various terminologies used in cooking; I learn the difference between sautéing and blanching, and the julienne style of chopping vegetables. I also learn how in Chinese cooking, cutting the vegetables with precision is the most important thing, and how it has to be cooked on very high flame for very little time.

Baiju has already cooked for the day and left. But I badly want to cook, to try out all that I have learnt in my cooking class. I zero in on a sumptuous-sounding Chinese meal and decide to go shopping for the ingredients I would need. When I finally make it, I am so pleased with the results. The fried rice and noodles are cooked to perfection. So are the stir-fried vegetables in hot garlic sauce. And so is the chilly–garlic chicken. I am so darn proud of my first home-cooked meal that I simply sit and gaze at it in admiration. It looks so professional for a first timer! Maybe I do have my mother's natural flair for cooking. In a strange way, I feel connected to my mother, and it has been ages since I have thought of her.

I feel so happy that I immediately call up Samir to tell him of my culinary achievement. He listens and then says that it is a good thing, but he is in an important meeting and will get back to me later. I apologize and tell him that there is a lot of food and I would like to call my friends over to celebrate. He distractedly agrees.

I have been in touch with Chetana and Akash ever since I got back from Seychelles. I now feel a kind of special bond with them because they actually made so much effort to be with me throughout my wedding, playing the part of my family.

I call them and insist that they come to my home straight from work and that I will not take a 'no' for an answer.

'But, Nisha, it will take us at least one and a half hours to get to your place from Andheri,' says Chetana.

'So when did distance become an issue to visit an old friend? Get Akash and just come!' I order.

'He has his tennis practice and you know how important that is for him.'

'Tell him I said I will get very upset if he doesn't come and that he can give up his tennis for just one day.'

Finally they arrive. I squeal in joy as I open the door and hug them. It is the first time I am meeting them after my marriage. They are completely impressed with my home, just as I was when I had stepped into this house with Samir, for the first time all those months ago. It is now my home too. They can't stop raving about the house, the skylight, the view of the ocean, the airy balconies, the well done-up interiors, and the location.

'Nisha, you are so darn lucky to be living here!' exclaims Akash. Chetana too is undisguised in her admiration and oohs and aaahs at appropriate places, as I give them a walking tour of my home.

Samir watches us with an amused look on his face. He has come a little earlier than usual.

I have set the table well and it looks very attractive with placemats and the tablecloth and cutlery neatly arranged. (Table setting is a part of the course as well, and I am a proud student today.) Chetana and Akash just cannot believe that I have done all the cooking. Akash asks me to confess whether I got it from a restaurant. I tell them about my cooking course and how much I am enjoying it.

They talk about Parinita, how she has become even stricter than before. Akash says he is preparing hard for the CAT exam en route to an MBA. He says his goal is to get into one of the IIMs, the most coveted management institutes in the country, and that that the job at Point to Point is only temporary. Chetana talks about the latest parade of men in her arranged-marriage chapter. She says that she has met about four IIT graduates so far, and each one turned out to be crazier than the last. She says most of them are selfish pricks and have no idea of how to talk to a woman. She talks about how most are so scared that they are not 'cool enough' and she talks about how unfit they all are, and how they have no sense of what to wear, and how they have this superior attitude and think they are smarter than most people around.

Akash cleverly refuses to comment but he winks at me and says 'Yeah, non-IIT guys are cooler any day' and then he asks Samir about his education and says sheepishly, 'I hope you are not from IIT.'

Samir politely says that he has gone to Wharton, before which he went to Hughes Hall, Cambridge. Samir's educational qualifications are as blue-blooded as they can get. Akash does not know what to say, but he is clearly in awe of Samir now.

'It must be really expensive to study in those places, right?' asks Chetana.

I feel a little embarrassed. Samir comes from money. For their family, it wouldn't really be as 'expensive' as Chetana puts it. I wonder what made Chetana make a comment like that. It's not as though her folks aren't wealthy. But I suppose, if Samir is royalty here, she is perhaps not even a minor nobleman.

What are you and Akash then, Nisha? Commoners?

I hate myself even as I think that thought. Since when did I start classifying friends according to the wealth of their families? I quickly squash the thought and change the topic as it starts making me feel increasingly uncomfortable.

'Hey, what is Deepti up to nowadays?' I ask, deliberately changing the topic.

Chetana talks about Deepti and Prashant. She talks about how they are the only ones at Point to Point who will stick around till the end. She says she is also planning to leave the agency soon.

Samir does not talk much at all. I badly want to show him off. I want my friends to think of him as charming, clever, and down-to-earth, the qualities I most admire in him. I badly want him to impress my friends. But he has withdrawn into polite silence and answers mostly in monosyllables, even when they try to draw him into our conversations. Akash, Chetana, and I carry on the cheerful banter, but I am beginning to feel very uncomfortable at how Samir is interacting with them.

They, of course, have no clue of the slightly substandard treatment that Samir is meting out to them, and they presume he is taciturn and reserved.

No sooner than they leave, Samir says 'phew' as he exhales sharply.

I am too angry with him to speak. But I cannot keep quiet and I blurt out.

'Look Samir, if you did not want my friends to come, you should have said so in the first place. You were so withdrawn all through the meal, making me feel like you were condescending towards them.'

'Did you ask if I wanted to socialize with them?'

'Come on! What is to ask? I did mention it to you on the phone when you were in a meeting.'

'You know how I am when I am working. Nothing you said really registered.'

I am upset and I keep quiet.

'See, it was different when you were working there. You have moved on in life, Nisha. You are now Mrs Samir Sharma. I cannot really relate to all the talk about your internal Point to Point politics, nor does it interest me in the least. I do find both of them a little immature, and come on—we are at a different level from where they are.'

'Samir,' I say, slowly emphasizing each word, 'they are my *friends*. And they are the only ones I have.'

'Look Nisha, I have had a hard day at work. The last thing I want to do when I come home is entertain people. Heck, why am I even having this conversation with you?'

I had marched out angrily and shut the bedroom door and then made that entry in my journal. That had been our first fight.

And the first time we had make-up sex too. I realized what it meant only when I experienced it.

Soon after, I was pregnant with our first child. I was thrilled, ecstatic, and overjoyed to discover it.

Samir had not wanted a baby.

That perhaps was the first wedge, the first crack which appeared in our relationship. But the joy of pregnancy, the joy of a new journey, the excitement of such a big event, overrode everything else.

I was going to become a mother and that was all that mattered to me.

Nisha's journals

2001

December 25th

Discovered that I am expecting. (OH MY GOD, I am going to be a mother!) The due date of the baby (My baby! My very own baby!) is August 5, 2002. I am truly overjoyed. I still do not know how I could have completely forgotten to take the pill. Was it because of a subconscious desire in me to become a mother? I don't know. All I know is that I am ecstatically happy. I have never known such joy in my life!

But Samir can be so unreasonable at times. I was really upset when he suggested I have an abortion. I know he is not fond of children. I know he did not want to become a father so soon. But heck, it has happened now. I do think destiny has given us a gift, and we should joyfully accept.

I have assured Samir that I will do every single thing on my own when the baby comes. I will wake up in the night, I will care for him/her. I will be there 24x7 and truly will not bother him.

I am very excited about my pregnancy. And I miss my mother like crazy. I did feel a little bad that I have absolutely nobody of my own to share this joy with other than Samir, and he is being such a wet blanket about this whole thing.

I am happy Chetana and Akash share my joy.

Chetana is getting married in June, which means I will be seven months pregnant then! She made me promise that I will attend the wedding.

Akash is happy for me, but I found it a bit strange when he asked if I am absolutely sure that this is what I want.

Of course this is what I want. I am going to be a MOTHER. I am going to shower my baby with all my love. I am going to give my baby everything that I never had as a child. I will be the BEST mother in the world. Akash laughed when I told him all this. I was beyond ecstatic to care.

But what does he know?

I am overjoyed. And I thank you God/Universe or whoever it is who controls our destines. Thank you!

The next entry in the journal is on June 13, 2002 (the day of Chetana's marriage).

Attended Chetana's wedding today. Samir was too busy with work. He was travelling and could not come. Akash was there, though.

Chetana looked radiant as a bride. I could see the glow on her face. I am glad she eventually found her Mr Right (and for the record, a non-IITian). She still hasn't got over the IIT bashing that she used to do, and she even joked about it today, just before going into the mandap, and we laughed about it as she made me agree that non-IIT guys are way cooler. She is her usual crazy self and not at all the demure bride I expected her to be!

I am glad my pregnancy is really easy. I have not experienced any of the horrors of pregnancy that Chetana keeps talking about. I like the way Akash treated me today. He was fussing over me, getting me a chair to sit on, asking if he can get me nimbu paani, and constantly enquiring if I was okay. It made me smile to see how much he cared.

I am so lucky to have such good friends in Chetana and Akash.

Chetana is going for her honeymoon to Koh Samui. I am really happy for her.

Akash says he is very well prepared for the CAT exam this year and the moment he gets in, he will quit working at Point to Point.

I saw Prashant too at the wedding. He came over and said a polite hello and congratulated me on my pregnancy. I just smiled. There is such a lot of difference between him and me now. I can't even imagine how I could have ever been excited to go out on a date with him! I have grown so much in this one year. All I can do is wish him well.

I am tired now. Today has been a really hectic day and I must rest.

I am content and happy though, and I think I just felt my baby kick!

I sigh as I remember that time vividly. Journals really have a way of reviving long-forgotten memories. I even remember the clothes Akash had worn that day. I had complimented him, telling him that he looked really good in Indian attire, and I found it amusing to see him blushing. I smile as I recollect that incident. I then make myself a cup of tea and settle down in my father's easy chair, the one he used to always read newspapers in and I continue reading the next entry my journal.

Sacred Heart Hospital, Mumbai

2002

August 7th

I am still in a lot of pain and still in a daze after the delivery. All that makes it worthwhile is my darling daughter's face as she sleeps. She was born yesterday evening, and I haven't slept a wink after she was born. I am exhausted, but am not able to sleep at all! She took a full six and a half hours to come out! Thank Lord it was a normal delivery. The gynaecologist had said that if she did not come out by 6.40 p.m., they would have to do a C-section emergency operation. That petrified me. After going through all this, I really did not want a C-section.

My stitches still hurt. There are a total of eight stitches from the delivery. They had to cut a little down there to give the baby enough headspace to come out.

I am still in a daze. But I am gradually learning how to carry her and how to let her suckle. It is getting her to burp that I find a tad bit difficult, but I am sure with time, I will get the hang of it too. I love the little crib I have got for her. I love her room, I love how she smells, I just love every single thing about her. She is my angel, my joy!

It does feel a bit bad that Samir has not even carried her and was not even present for the delivery. He came only this morning, and did not even bother kissing me like he always does after returning from a business trip. I badly wanted him to hold me and tell me how happy he is for the both of us. But he did nothing of that sort. He just gave Tanya a cursory glance (yeah, I have already decided the name and Samir says he is fine with whatever name I choose,) and then said he had to make an important call to the UK to check on his mother, as she was not well and had to be taken to the hospital.

2002

August 13th

Samir's mother passed away last night. Samir wants me to go with him to London for the funeral. How can I?

I can barely manage to sit up straight. My stitches still hurt. Tanya is awake every two hours. I have to keep cleaning her, keep feeding her.

He says we will fly business class. As if that can take care of the pain! Why, even the paediatrician strictly advised me against travelling with a baby who is not even ten days old. Why is it only Samir who fails to understand?

I close my journal with a sigh. Chetana had come to visit me the day Samir had left for UK.

In those pregnancy-induced, hormone-crazy days, I used to be quite emotional. I was overwhelmed seeing Chetana and had cried a bucketful in front of her.

She had some news for me as well. She was pregnant too!

'Hey, how was the delivery? Is it bad?' she asked apprehensively.

'Well, it's like shitting a watermelon,' I had laughed.

'Yuck, gross! Don't you have any other way to describe it?'

'You wanted to know! I didn't volunteer,' I had smiled.

Then Chetana wanted a blow-by-blow account of everything that happened when I was in the delivery room. She kept asking questions and listening intently to whatever I had to say. Just two years ago, it was she who had been instructing me on what to wear and how to land a date. And here I was, lecturing her about motherhood and pregnancy. How things change.

Chetana had found it very appalling that Samir had not been present for the delivery, and that he had left me all alone with a baby.

'Come on, Chetana, His mother has died,' I said, defending him.

'Yeah, I agree, but it was unfair of him to expect you to go along. Those who have died have gone. Here is a small life totally dependent on you. And what about YOU, Nisha? What about your pain? Your stitches?'

I had argued with her and staunchly defended Samir. I had told her that just because Samir was different from her husband in certain aspects, it did not mean that he loved me any less. It was just that he was uncomfortable around babies and children.

Chetana had left it at that, but I could see that she was not convinced.

Akash had come two days later. I was moved to see how he held Tanya. He was so careful with her, tenderly lifting her, and planting a kiss on her cheek. He then cradled her in his arm and stroked her head.

He looked at me with his eyes shining and an expression

of reverence and awe on his face and whispered, 'God, she is so tiny and so perfect.'

Seeing Akash hold her so tenderly was a totally emotional moment for me. Samir had not even held her. And here was Akash showering so much love. Again, I promptly burst into tears at this tender display of affection and hastily wiped my eyes.

Akash was too engrossed in Tanya and too absorbed to notice.

I stood there transfixed, looking at the two of them, lost in their own world. Akash was cooing to Tanya and Tanya was being so soothed by his voice.

An unwanted thought crawled into my mind like a stealthy urchin sneaking off with a loaf from a baker's cart. A thought which said, 'If only Akash was the father of the baby; they are so perfect together.'

I had no idea then how this little seed of a thought, which had sprouted like a puny weed, would come back years later, like a thick forest of tall trees, to surround me with shadows of a life-altering choice I would have to make. I had gazed at the both of them for a long time that day, too afraid to move, in case I disturbed the serenity.

It was only after he left that I realized that for the first time in many years, I had experienced something so strange, an emotion I had never felt before. It was hard to put a name to feeling, but it was so blissful, so calming, and so soothing, that I found myself craving for it again.

I Can't Make You Love Me

Present day

Mumbai

The enormity of the situation that I am currently in does not strike me till Tanya announces that she wants to go to Naturals Parlour for some ice cream. She has just come from school, and baby Rohit and I have greeted her as usual at the gate of our apartment complex where her school bus drops her off.

'Mama, can we go for ice creams? Please, please, please?' she pleads as soon as she sees me.

Rohit gurgles happily on seeing her and makes a lunge towards her.

'Please, Mama, can I carry him?' she asks, the earlier request of ice cream now forgotten. Without even waiting for my reply, she hands over her school bag to me and stretches her arms towards him. This excites him even further, and he almost leaps out of my arms towards her. He is getting heavier and heavier by the day, and after carrying him for just ten minutes, my arms start hurting. He cannot walk yet, but he crawls really fast, and this is an awkward stage, because I cannot place him anywhere while I wait for Tanya's bus to arrive. He has to be in my arms all the time, as he has learnt how to stand up in his pram, and he yells if I try to strap him down.

'Tanya, he is heavy now. You will not be able to carry him,' I try to reason, but my little girl has a mind of her own and she has already decided what she wants. She usually gets it.

'Come on, Mama, I can carry him. I am nearly eight,' she proudly says as she carries him. I watch like a hawk, in case he gets too heavy for her and they trip over, but she manages perfectly.

My heart fills with maternal pride as I watch them both. Two perfect children. My two angels. How I adore them.

She manages to carry him till the elevator when he lunges towards the buttons.

'No, no, Rohit. You're a baby. Tanya will do it for you,' she says, taking charge breezily, with a confident assurance of innocence which only a child can have.

Then she remembers the ice creams again.

'Mama, can we go for ice creams now? I badly, badly want one today, mama,' she says again, her eyes shining. She has her father's looks and his charms. Her shoulder-length straight hair, which she inherited from her dad, make her look like a doll, and it is hard to refuse when she pleads like that with her expressive eyes.

'Okay, go change first, and let me get Rohit ready too, after which we will all go together,' I say.

'Yay, Mama! You are the best Mama in the whole world.' She gleams, running off happily to her room to change.

But I wasn't good enough for your dad, my baby.

I bite back my tears which seem to be coming without any warning, flowing at the slightest nudge, just like a leaky tap that has been fixed temporarily with a sticky tape.

Naturals ice cream parlour is just a short walk from our apartment.

At Naturals, my pain comes back threefold. I see two families there. One is a husband, a wife, and a toddler who is around two. The lady is obviously pregnant. The other is a family with two children, who are around twelve and fourteen. The husband tastes his ice cream, and the joy on his face is hard to miss, as he offers the cone to his wife and says, 'Try this, this is really nice.' She takes a lick of his cone, hands it back, and smiles as she says, 'Try mine now, it is really nice too.'

That simple gesture feels like someone is grinding the shards of glass left in my heart with a heavy army boot, grinding them in really hard. I wince and bite my lip.

I watch them, thinking how Samir and I would have been somewhat like this couple in a few years, only if he had stayed. That had always been my dream, to have a happy family, a *complete* family, something that I had never had as a child. Was that too much to ask?

Tanya is oblivious to my inner turmoil, as she happily slurps the choco-walnut ice cream cone, her favourite flavour.

'Mama, when will Daddy come back from Germany?' she asks as she takes another lick.

She is blissful, content, and happy in her childhood, a childhood which is about to change forever, because two people, two mature adults who were once in love with each other, have screwed up somewhere.

Sorry, your papa has left me, and we cannot be a happy family anymore, but here, have an ice cream.

Stop it Nisha, you do not want to cry in front of your children and make a scene at the ice cream parlour; for heaven's sake! Stop it right now.

I manage to swallow the lump in my throat and tell her it may be a while.

It is only when I walk back with the children, that something strikes me—I have only three thousand rupees left in my purse. Samir is the one who usually hands me money as and when I need it. I do have a bank account of my own, which I have not used for many years now. I had stopped using it the day I had married Samir.

I have an add-on credit card and have no clue if Samir has cancelled it. Panic sets in. I need to talk to Samir. I need to talk to him *now.* I want to ask him about the financial arrangements.

There is only a small problem.

No matter how many times I call, Samir does not answer his phone.

I do not know what to do about the money situation. I send a text message to Samir. It just says to call me as I need to talk to him. I wait for two hours. Then I text him again saying I wanted to talk to him about the money situation (just in case he thinks I want to rant and rave, which I very much want to do, but the more important thing here is to get the finances in order first).

There is no reply. The children have been given their dinner. Tanya now insists that I read her a bedtime story. It is a little ritual that we have. I read her a story, tuck her in, kiss her, and turn off the lights and head off. This is a time Tanya looks forward to as her exclusive time with me, after Rohit has slept. She has my undivided attention all to herself.

But today, my mind wanders off thrice while reading *The Girl with the Broken Wing* to her. It is a book by Heather Dyer and is one of Tanya's favourites. Even though Tanya can read all by herself and can read very well too, she still enjoys our little daily ritual of reading.

Finally, when I stop midway through a sentence, Tanya gets exasperated and takes out the book from my hand.

'Mama, you are not paying attention today, I will read it myself.'

'Sorry, baby,' I say, as I sit there stupidly listening to my little girl reading out *The Girl with the Broken Wing*. That is exactly how I feel.

Broken and shattered. I am the girl with the broken wing.

And two children.

When Tanya finishes her chapter, I tell her it is time to sleep and kiss her goodnight.

I sit on the balcony and stare at the moon.

What am I going to do? I do need to speak to Samir. I call him, my heart pounding when the phone rings.

He does not answer it again. I call three more times and finally, the call is picked up.

By Maya.

'Uh, hello Nisha,' she mutters.

I picture Samir and Maya in bed. The thought is too much to bear. A mixture of disgust, jealousy, anger, resentment, and hurt fills my soul. It travels through my bloodstream, like slow, molten lava. It makes me blind with rage and pure helplessness. I want to scream at her. And at him. I want to go to whichever place they both are in and I really want to kill them both. I would always read about crimes of passion in the newspapers and wonder why such crimes were committed. Now I know. That is exactly what I want to do right now. But I have no way of knowing where they are, and besides, I have the children. So my burning need for revenge remains just that—a helpless longing, lashing deep inside me, burning me out from the inside. I am like a butterfly trapped in a glass jar whose life force is ebbing out. The lid is tightly shut and there is no escape.

I go to our bedroom and put the pillow against my face, screaming loudly. The pillow muffles the sound. I scream again and again. It is a primeval cry for help. Nobody can hear me except myself. Even at that heightened state of anguish, somewhere my sanity reminds me that the children are asleep and should not be woken up.

I pace up and down furiously in our bedroom. Exhausted and trapped, I climb into bed, but I am unable to sleep. The night stretches long ahead of me. In the past, no matter what has happened, I have always slept soundly at night. But now, sleep just evades me.

Finally, when I am unable to toss and turn anymore, I go to the kitchen and make myself a large cup of hot chocolate.

Then I go to the desktop and log in to my mail. I have a habit of checking my mail once in three to four days. I usually get only forwards and spam messages. But today when I open my inbox, my heart starts beating at a thousand beats per minute.

There is a mail from Samir staring at me from the computer screen.

Leaving on a Jet Plane

Nisha,

There is a lot I want to say, but I do not know where to begin. I am going to be honest with you here. I wish I could say the usual line, 'It's not you, but me'. But I cannot do that. You have indeed changed a lot in the past eight years. You are no longer the person you were when we first met each other. We have grown apart, and what I feel is so darn pathetic is that you have not even realized it.

I agree I have changed too, but what hurts most is that you were too busy to even notice.

We indeed had a good thing going in the beginning. But where it started going sour, I really cannot pinpoint. Maybe it was when you told me you were pregnant with Tanya. I had made my views clear then, Nisha, hadn't I? You had told me you were on birth control and you had assured me it was safe. We both had agreed that if at all we had children, we would have them only after six to seven years, when we both felt ready. But then you got pregnant, and sometimes I wondered if it was a kind of deliberate ploy on your part to tie me down. Even when I had told you that I had no interest whatsoever in being a father (maybe I am different from most people, I do not know), you still went ahead and decided to keep the baby, hoping that once the baby was born, I would change my viewpoint, even when I have been constantly telling you that having a baby at that point is indeed a disruption in my life.

For five years after that, I watched in silence as my house slowly changed. From being spotless and perfectly clean, it went to being filled with toys and discarded diapers, and baby powder, and shampoo, and what not. Our sex life became totally non-existent. I had absolutely no interest in Lamaze class or decorating the nursery. I had made that clear too. But you would nag on endlessly until I consented to going with you to them, where the instructor told you how to breathe, while other proud fathers tried to bond with each other. God—I loathed and hated all of it. Even when I voiced it, you brushed my protests aside—so focussed were you on your needs, your wants.

I know you had your differences with my mother. But when you refused to come with me to London for her funeral, it was truly a huge blow for me. Yes, I know Tanya was only twelve days old, and you were still feeding her, but we would have anyway flown first class, not even business class. The dead do deserve some respect, Nisha. It would have meant the world to me if you had even made a tiny bit of effort to accompany me. But the way you so flatly refused, and the way you made it sound as though my asking you to accompany me was utter drivel, that was what really hit me hard.

You know how business has grown so rapidly over the past few years and the time when the Singapore branch was being set up. There was so much work pressure on me then, and when I came home at night, it was to a house where I did not even dare ask for a cup of tea for fear of being snubbed, as you were too tired from looking after the baby (which you yourself were so keen on bringing into the world in the first place). And no, I did not mind making that cup of tea for you, provided you cheerfully accepted it. But no—you were grumpy, irritated, and moody most of the time—maybe stress, maybe exhaustion—I do not know.

And how can I forget the sleepless nights.

Just as we settled down to bed, the baby would wail, and you insisted on keeping her crib in our bedroom. There are thousands of parents who have a nursery for their babies, and it is perfectly fine—but no, you felt it was cruel. Still I gave in, I consented.

I longed to discuss the developments at the newly opened Singapore branch with you, but all you had to talk about was which shop was selling diapers cheaper and which shop was holding a sale for baby merchandise. And then your litany of woes about the live-in help we hired, you had nothing to talk about except how she was not good at her work, and finally you threw her out saying only you are good enough, and that she is incompetent to raise your precious babies.

Your presence was needed at all the official dinners where I met my business partners. You could have contributed majorly and proved an asset to me. But whenever I asked you to accompany me, you made up excuses involving the baby. Either she had her vaccines, or she was not well, or she had to be fed, or she was throwing up, or something of that sort.

Slowly I stopped asking you, stopped discussing business with you altogether.

You even had problems with almost all my friends whom you said were too stuck up and high class. You refused to accompany me to Dev and Vini's party. You did not want to attend Ranjit's farmhouse bash. Heck, you did not even want to come with me to a pub for a casual night out, and I have asked you so many times. Even when I had planned that trip to the discotheque (the night when I had also arranged for a babysitter and got the invites as a surprise), you created such a fuss. I began fearing asking my friends over because you deeply disapproved. I threw myself into work to forget about all of it. I had a good set of friends and a good social life. But you ensured that it all came to a grinding halt.

I have worked really hard to give you this lifestyle. Every single year, we have holidayed abroad. We have stayed at the best of places and gone to the most exotic locations. But there too, you hardly came out of the hotel room, hardly got into the water or did anything remotely fun, saying Tanya was too small and it was her nursing time. All the time, Nisha, and I do mean all the time, it was Tanya this, Tanya that.

It was as though I ceased to exist for you after Tanya was born, being relegated to the role of merely the money provider.

On the rare occasions that we had sex too, it was always hurried. You were so disinterested and half the time, your ears were on high alert to hear whether Tanya would wake up. You could not stop worrying even while having sex?!

And then it happened a second time around. How in the world can a same mistake happen TWICE, Nisha? Again you assured me that it was okay and that you were taking the pills. How then, I would like to know, did Rohit happen?

And we went through the same cycle again; the only difference was that now it was with two kids instead of one.

Never once did you bother to ask what I want out of all of this.

You were happy being a total mother. I kept quiet all this while for the sake of maintaining peace in the house. You did not seem to care that I was slogging my butt off to provide you the comfort you have so got used to. You don't even have a clue about the Singapore office project and how much it means to me.

My house seems to have turned into a goddamn nursery, with kids walking in and out all the time, and on weekends, when I most want to relax and chill out in front of the television with a beer, there would be Tanya's friends, ringing the bell, creating a ruckus as usual.

I think life is too short to not grab what you want out of it. I truly cannot live like this, where I yearn for even five minutes of peace. If after working so hard, I cannot have that much, I really think it is not worth it.

Then of course, all the travel which the new project involves, all the deals we did, it was Maya who played a big role in helping to make it happen. She has been around for me, and she is indeed a smart woman. I am in love with her now and she is with me.

Look, I know you need money. I will pay for the kids' education and will give you a good sum for your monthly expenses. Please activate your bank account. Please apply for your own ATM cards and credit cards. Let me know the account number and I will transfer the desired amount to your bank account.

I am sorry this might have come as a rude wake-up call, but this was the only way to break it to you. Maya and I have been growing closer and closer over the last one and a half years. You were too self-involved to even notice or ask me. Now, isn't that unusual?

Think about it and text me your bank account number.

Samir

I read it, each sentence hitting me with the force of a gale wind. I read it with my fists clenched. I read it with tears welling up in my eyes. I read it biting my lip. I read it once, and then I read it again.

Out of all the things he stated, two things seemed to have pierced my very soul. He had said 'MY house' and 'YOUR precious babies'.

Gosh, how could he? When I had refused to accompany him for his mother's funeral, it was because I had stitches between my vagina and anus, and they hurt like hell—I could not even sit up, unless it was on a special cushion. How could he not understand my physical pain? And there was the newborn baby's constant need to suckle. I had not slept five nights at a stretch—it had been such a hard labour where he had not even bothered to come into the delivery room. Yet, I did not complain once.

I read it once more and his words make me feel like a worthless piece of shit. I feel truly terrible about the foreign vacations (which he insisted we go on, as the company paid for a package once a year). If he was this unhappy in our marriage, why in the world had he kept silent so far?

I feel so angry and so hurt that I wished I had a truckload of money to go and throw on his face, to pay him back for having stayed in HIS house and raising MY kids. I am blinded with fury, hurt by the injustice of his words.

Everything always has two sides. I am completely shocked at the side he saw and the side he has chosen to believe. The way I had been seeing it was totally different. I had accepted him as a part of 'US'. I had never even thought of him as only the 'provider'. I had presumed that he did not talk about work because he had indeed mentioned it on various occasions how he prefers to leave all his worries back at work and not bring them home.

I had thought that by handling all of Tanya's and Rohit's needs on my own, I had been giving him the space he needs. By not asking for his help when it came to kids, I had presumed that he would get his time to do his work, and that he would appreciate my taking care of every single thing at home.

I look around this place which I have called 'home' for the past eight years. With each passing second, the walls of the house with the colour-coordinated paintings on them seem to be mocking me. With each passing second, all the expensive things in the house—the fixtures, the furnishings, which I had not even given a second thought to, now seem to be telling me that I am not worthy of them.

I feel cheated and betrayed. I feel insulted. But most of all, I just feel like an idiot who has climbed on to a wrong bus, thinking that it is going to Disneyland, when in fact it is headed to the junkyard.

Let him keep HIS precious house. All I want are MY two precious babies. Yes, my children mean the world to me. I know the bitter pain of growing up without a mother. All I had wanted to do was to give my children a great childhood and a mother's affection, both of which I had been denied as a child. I had naturally been overjoyed to finally have my own children. How could I abort, just because he was not ready? Since when did wanting to raise your own children and shower them with love become such a crime?

I know right then that I cannot live in this house for even a minute more. I know what to do. I have made up my mind.

I tiptoe slowly to the children's room. I use a wooden stool and take down the three large suitcases stored in the cupboard space above the walk-in closet. Then I meticulously pack all their stuff. I drag the suitcases to my bedroom and pack all my clothes in. I pack my journal too, which has been my lifeline whenever it was hard to cope. I also pack the most important of the children's toys, the ones they absolutely cannot do without. My calmness surprises me.

Finally, I call up dial-a-cab and book a taxi.

Alone in a Crowd

It is nearly midnight when I make this life-altering decision. When the cab arrives, I request the driver to come upstairs and carry the suitcases to the cab. I wake up Tanya who is bleary-eyed and dazed. She has no idea why she is being woken up in the middle of the night. Rohit is fast asleep and does not even stir when I carry him.

'Mama, I want to sleep. Where are we going now?' asks Tanya groggily, barely making sense as she mutters.

'Shhh, baby. We have to go. Come quietly please,' I reply.

Tanya is too dazed to even protest, and she follows meekly behind me, as the cab driver loads our stuff into the cab.

I have only a vague idea of what I am doing. But I do know that staying for even a minute more in that house would have been oppressive. I truly cannot bear being there after reading Samir's mail.

The children fall asleep in the cab almost immediately, and I give the cab driver the address of my old flat, which was where I had been living when Samir had first walked into my life. I have not been to that place for more than a year now. The last I had visited was before Rohit was born. After my father passed away and I got married, I had initially wanted to give it out on rent. But Samir had insisted that it was too much trouble for the pittance of a rent it would fetch.

It still had all the furniture, the beds, and the implements in the kitchen. I would visit the flat about two or three times each year and get it cleaned. Then I would spend a little time in my old room, reminiscing about how much life had changed for me. Occasionally, a memory would glisten like a drop of dew on a rosebud in the early morning. I would pause and soak it in, memories full of loneliness and pain and years of being ignored by my father, as I secretly nursed my dreams and hopes, disguising it with a big, fake smile, and carried on as if nothing mattered. No one could tell.

Samir had come along and changed all that. My life had taken such an upward spiral when he had entered it, it was as though somebody had pressed a button on the elevator to the penthouse and it had zoomed non-stop ever since.

Except that the elevator, the penthouse, and everything else had been fake, like a movie set. I had nothing now, except my two children.

There is barely any traffic on the road at this time of the night and the driver zooms at breakneck speed. I don't even feel like telling him to slow down. Like little

Tanya, I am also too dazed to care. We reach my old apartment in exactly twenty-two minutes and the cab driver assists me in getting the luggage out.

As I pay him his fare, I find myself mentally counting the amount of money left in my purse and I hate it. Since my marriage to Samir, I have never ever been in a situation like this, and it pinches me. When Tanya is woken up again the second time that night, she starts protesting loudly and crying.

'Hush, my baby, hush. You can sleep now, nobody will disturb you,' I say, as I lead her to the double bed in what used to be my father's room. She climbs on to the bed, collapses, and falls asleep almost instantly. One of the perks of being a child is the ability to fall asleep so quickly, free of any worries. I place baby Rohit beside her. I look at the innocent, trusting faces of both my children and I feel a pain that I have never felt before. It is the pain of being rejected, being betrayed, being kicked in the gut by a person you gave your heart and soul to.

The person who is the father of my children.

Most of my life, I have trusted my impulses and my instinct, and it has taken me along. My decision to move into this home too was made in a spilt of a second.

Just like the decision I had made to kiss Samir on the moonlight beach in Bali all those years ago.

I grit my teeth, fighting back the tears. I feel devastated, but I do not want to cry yet again. I have done enough crying for the night.

I toss and turn and keep replaying the contents of Samir's letter in my head. I wince with the fresh wave of hurt that strikes deep. I feel like a prisoner being tortured and hit from the back with arms tied, without knowing where the next blow will land. I desperately want to turn off Samir's thoughts, his words. I want to block him out. I do not want to think about it. But it is as though a demon has gripped me in his clutch and is taunting me. A thousand thoughts swirl around in my head. Why didn't Samir at least try once to make matters right? I hate Maya with every pore, every cell in my body, even though I know it is not solely her fault.

Rohit stirs in his sleep, and this brings me back to earth, forces me to stop thinking about Samir. Suddenly I realize that the first thing in the morning Rohit would want his milk. I remember that there is nothing in the house. I panic for a few minutes. How foolish of me to walk out of the house in the middle of the night with two children in tow? How terribly immature and silly of me. Yet, when I think of Samir's words, I know I cannot bear the thought of staying there even for a few seconds and feel I have done the right thing by walking out.

I take a deep breath and force myself to calm down. I decide to stay awake and ring the doorbell of the person who lives in the opposite flat as soon as it is dawn. I have no idea who lives there, but I decide that whoever it is, I would explain my situation and ask to borrow a glass of milk. Surely that would not be a problem?

Then I think about Tanya's school. She always goes by the school bus, and I know that the school bus does come to this area too. I decide that there is no point in Tanya missing her school, just because her parents are busy messing up their lives. I decide that as soon as it is around 7.30 a.m. (which I figure will be a decent hour), I would call the assigned bus-teacher and ask her where the pickup point for children in this area would be, and also whether it would be possible to pick up Tanya from here on a daily basis.

I feel calmer having solved two immediate and practical problems and then set about unpacking the stuff I have carried in my suitcase, putting it away methodically, simply to distract myself from the pain of Samir's actions. Also, Tanya would require her school uniform the next day. The faster this place feels like home, the better it is for all of us.

I cannot help but feel like I am in a dump of a place after the opulence of my previous home.

Samir's home, Nisha, not yours. He stated it himself.

The painful realization feels like I have inadvertently touched a burning ember. How can someone you consider your own, end something like this, a meaningful marriage without so much as an iota of guilt? How can someone walk out on his wife and children? I am angry and upset all over again, but I control myself as I hear a noise outside the flat. I glance at the clock and am surprised to see it is nearly 5.40 a.m. I go to the balcony, the same balcony where I stood all those years ago, as I waited, watching out for Samir's car the day my father passed away. I peer down and see the milk-delivery man unloading the crates of milk from his bicycle. This is good, as it means that I don't have to ring my neighbour's doorbell for milk.

I open the door to my flat and wait for him to come by. When he is keeping the milk packets in the jute bag left on the door opposite by my neighbour, I call out to him.

'Madam, doodh roz chahiye? Coupon doon?' he asks.

I tell him that I would indeed require milk every day. I ask him how much the coupons cost and hand over the amount. And then he tells me that he supplies bread and fresh eggs too and asks if I want those. I am happy at this stroke of luck and I bless him silently, as it means that my immediate need of catering to Tanya's breakfast is taken care of.

Just as I am shutting the door to my flat, clutching the packet of milk, bread, and eggs, I see an old lady opening the door of the flat opposite to mine. She is short, with wrinkled skin, bobbed white hair, thick glasses, and is wearing a kind of a frock. She also has a hearing aid.

'Hello, dear. Have you newly moved in?' she calls out cheerfully.

'Yes, just last night,' I reply, not wanting to make conversation, hoping that she would take a hint that I have just moved in and hence I am busy. In reality, it is just that I do not want any nosy neighbours, and especially old ladies, offering opinion on my current situation, which I feel she is most likely to do.

'How wonderful to finally have a neighbour! This flat was locked for so long. Do come over if you need anything,' she continues chirpily (a bit too chirpily for my liking). I simply nod and thank her while shutting the door.

When I turn around, I find that Tanya has woken up and is rubbing her eyes and looking around as though she is in a dream and cannot believe where she is. Despite all my worries, I find myself smiling as I gaze at her puzzled face.

I keep the eggs, milk, and bread on the dining table and give her a hug, carrying her to the sofa and plonking down with her in my lap.

'How is your new house, baby? Like it?' I ask.

'Why have we come here, Mama? How did we come?' she asks.

She obviously was too disoriented to remember her midnight taxi-ride.

'Mama will explain all this in the evening. You have to go to school now. Which reminds me, I have to call your bus teacher. You have a new bus route from today,' I say, as I dial the teachers' number.

Five minutes later, Tanya's travel arrangements are sorted out as the bus indeed crosses this route. The teacher has given instructions as to where it will stop and the names of two children in Tanya's class who board the bus from the same place. I know the bus stop well, as I have grown up in this area, and I know that it is a seven-minute walk from this apartment.

Tanya has seen me writing down the names of the children who will be in the same bus stop with her while I was speaking to her teacher.

'Maaa, Nikita and Sneha are going to be there! Maa, you know what? I sit next to Nikita in class. Nikita is Sneha's friend, but she can be my friend too. I will ask her,' says Tanya excitedly, sorting out the politics of friendship and diplomacy inside her head. I smile again at her unfazed enthusiasm. Oh, to be a child of seven!

Her biggest problem in life right now is how to wheedle herself in the friendship between Nikita and Sneha, and how to secure her position. The fact that her life has changed forever does not strike her at all, and I am happy for her innocence and her immediate acceptance of our new situation.

I tell her to get ready for school, and I am glad that she is old enough to have a bath on her own. 'Mama, where is my uniform? she asks.

'In the cupboard, baby. Mama has unpacked it. Look, this section of the wardrobe is all yours, the other section is Mama's, and this third section here is Rohit's,' I say, as I open the wardrobe and show her how I have neatly organized the clothes.

'But Rohit has only diapers and baby clothes,' Tanya giggles.

I am compelled to join her.

'Yeah, he is a such a baby. You are a big girl. You can even have a bath on your own,' I say.

'And also brush my hair, don't forget,' she adds.

I boil the milk and busy myself with preparing breakfast. I am thankful that Tanya's school is one of those which supplies lunch to its students.

I check on Rohit and he is still asleep.

Tanya comes out fully dressed, looking really smart. For a seven-year-old, she is indeed efficient and independent.

'Mama, where are my school shoes?' she asks.

That is when I realize that I have forgotten to bring her school uniform shoes.

'Oh no, baby. Silly Mama! I have forgotten to bring your shoes. They are in the other house,' I say.

'What to do now, Mummy?' she asks in dismay.

'Wear your sandals today. I will write a note explaining to your class teacher, asking her to excuse you for today,' I say.

Tanya agrees happily to this suggestion too; for her it is the novelty involved—she can now wear sandals to school, something which she is not usually allowed to do.

I open Tanya's school diary and turn to the section of 'Parents' Notes to Teachers'.

I sit for a few minutes, poised with the pen in my hand, wondering how on earth to explain to her class teacher that I have hauled the kids to a different home in the middle of the night and hence forgotten the school shoes.

Finally I write: 'Ma'am, due to unavoidable circumstances, Tanya cannot wear her regular school shoes today. I request you to kindly excuse her for just today. She will be in the prescribed uniform tomorrow.'

Rohit has woken up now, and I give him milk which he happily slurps.

As I walk my daughter to her new bus-stop, in her school uniform and pink sandals, with my son perched happily on my hip, cooing at all the sights on the road, I wonder what in the world I am going to do with my life.

Tanya spots her friends and cheerfully calls out to them, telling them that from now on, she is on this bus route as she has shifted to a new house. They squeal in unison, the typical little-girls' squeal at otherwise trivial news which is so important and exciting for them.

I am surrounded by people, moving cars, traffic, school children, their mothers or fathers, and the busy Mumbai traffic.

Yet, for the very first time in my life, I feel all alone.

Every Rose Has Its Thorn

After Tanya leaves for school, I take Rohit and go to the supermarket nearby where I used to shop before marriage. I pick up the essential supplies and baby food and diapers for Rohit. Earlier when I shopped, I would never bother about the price. I would have loads of bags filled with grocery items, and the chauffur would carry the bags to the car. I would whip out my credit card (an add-on card to Samir's) and pay without so much as glancing at the bill. It would all go as smooth as silk, and a trip to go grocery shopping was something I enjoyed and looked forward to. I liked to see the new products, I liked to browse, compare ingredients in each of the products, and then make an informed choice. But today, I find myself comparing the prices. I have no clue if Samir has cancelled my add-on card. I don't want to be embarrassed at the counter in case I have no money to pay. I look into my wallet and I see that there is about twenty-two hundred rupees left. I do a quick mental addition and I see that my total bill is about nineteen-hundred rupees.

I walk to the cash counter, hand the cashier my card, clear my throat and say casually, 'Could you tell me if this card works? I think I might have got a wrong card. In case it doesn't work, I'll pay cash.' My heart is pounding as I say this well-thought-out speech, but the guy at the cash counter of course has no clue.

'Sure Ma'am, let me check,' he says politely as he swipes the card.

I wait with bated breath.

'Sorry Ma'am, it is not accepting the card. It says it has been cancelled.'

Even though I half expected it, it still feels like a huge slap.

'Oh, okay. No problem, I'll pay cash,' I say, as I carefully count out the notes.

For the very first time, I realize how it feels to be poor and to be without cash. I have just three hundred rupees left in my purse, but now my grocery supplies for at least two weeks has been taken care of. (I hope. I have no clue as I never kept a tab before on what I would buy and how long it is likely to last.)

'Can I have it kept in your car, madam?' offers the guy helpfully, glancing at Rohit perched on my hips.

I have no car and I have no money. My husband just cancelled my credit card too.

'Oh no, that's okay. I'll take it,' I smile bravely, as I lug the heavy bags in one arm, with baby Rohit still perched on my hips.

Once I reach home, I almost collapse with the effort of walking home with the bags and Rohit. My face and my whole body is covered in sweat. I am panting and puffing badly. But Rohit needs his bath. His bath time helps me calm down. It is a time which is just his and mine. It is a time he completely enjoys as he splashes in the water, giggling and chuckling. In the earlier house, he used to soak in the bathtub, but my father's apartment (now mine) has no such luxuries. Rohit does not mind the least bit and he laughs heartily, as I lower him into a large bucket filled with lukewarm water, testing it with my elbows, checking to make sure the water isn't too warm for him.

Once he is asleep, I rush to the kitchen and finish the cooking really fast. I discover that it feels so different when one is cooking just for oneself and two kids. When I was with Samir, making a meal was a long-drawn process, with three elaborate courses. The cook always made it well, but I mostly had to oversee. On the days I felt like cooking (after my cookery classes, I had enjoyed cooking so much that I had started cooking a lot, just to occupy my empty hours), I would give the cook an off, and make a proper three- or four-course meal, watching in quiet satisfaction as Samir ate. Samir could never tell the difference between what the cook had made and what I had. It did not bother me and in fact, I took it as a great compliment that I was as good as, if not better than, a professional cook.

'How is the dinner today?' I would ask, as I hovered around like a mother hen, watching Samir eat.

'Hmmm, it's really nice,' he would say in a distracted way, and I would smile a great big smile of happy satisfaction of a job well done.

At that time it did not matter, but bringing this memory up now hurts. It is like I have scratched a long-healed wound, in the hope of making a blister. Why I do this, I don't know. It is just that the pain of rejection has a funny way of grabbling people and kicking them again and again. The strange part is it is all self-inflicted, yet one is unable to break free.

I think about the time when we had invited his friends for dinner and I had cooked. I think about the time when I first knew I was pregnant. I think about the time Tanya had been born. I think about all the years that I have spent with him, and even though I do not want to cry, I end up crying again. I mentally kick myself and tell myself to get a grip. Why can't I let go and stop thinking about it?

How can you let go of eight years? How can something wonderful change into this?

When one has two small children, one cannot afford the luxury of thinking too much. Each day is a mad rush to simply get the routine chores done. With young children, you cannot afford to miss a meal, you simply cannot afford to miss a nap, and playtime and bath time are sacrosanct. In a way, I am happy for the routine. It keeps depressing thoughts at bay.

It's almost as though the children and I are in an isolated cocoon that we have created for ourselves. Tanya wakes up, gets ready for school, and I make her breakfast and mine too. Then I wake up Rohit, and we all march to the bus stop which is all but a six-minute walk from our flat. Tanya skips ahead and I hurry to keep pace with her, with Rohit perched on my hips. By the time I come back, I am huffing and puffing with the effort, usually drenched in sweat because of the humidity and the heat of the unrelenting Mumbai sunshine. But I do look forward to these walks to the bus stop, as they gives me a chance to get out of the house and get some fresh air. I am cautious of meeting other parents at the bus stop as I am not ready to give any explanations about my situation just yet. So I keep a distance and walk back with Rohit when Tanya boards the bus.

We do the same thing in the evening when the bus arrives. The time I am home, I mop and swab the house all by myself, as I would rather save on our already dwindling finances than employ a maid. I then bathe Rohit and finally have a bath myself. I am exhausted by the end of it all. On some days, Rohit's nap gets delayed, and some days it is so hectic that I would not have had a bath even till evening, when I go to greet Tanya at the bus stop. On those days, Tanya watches over Rohit, while I hurriedly have a bath.

It has been just about two weeks since we moved here, but we seem to have fallen into this familiar and comforting pattern. In a strange way, the drudgery of mundane housework is actually helping me cope with the tumultuous emotions which Samir's betrayal has created.

This little, insulated world we created for ourselves is disturbed one morning when the doorbell rings, just after I have come back from dropping Tanya to the bus stop. It is the old lady from across the floor. She is carrying a large glass bowl covered with aluminium foil in her arms.

'Good morning, dear! We haven't properly met. I am Mrs Billimoria,' she announces.

'Hello, Mrs Billimoria. I am Nisha,' I find myself speaking a little louder than necessary.

'I can hear you my dear, my hearing aid is on,' she smiles and points to it, and I am a little embarrassed at my presumption.

'So sorry,' I say, and then it seems a little silly to not invite her inside as I can see that is what she expects.

'Err...do you want to come in?' I ask, still a little hesitant to let anyone into our private little world.

'Thank you, my dear, I've got some Lagan Nu Custard for you. It is a Parsi sweet dish. I think your little children might enjoy it,' she says amiably, as she waddles slowly into my dining room (and into my life, but I am yet to know it then) and places the bowl of custard on my table.

I find the fact that she has thought about what my children would enjoy very endearing, and I am a little ashamed of my rather stand-offish behaviour so far, where I have studiously avoided her.

So I tell her that is indeed kind of her to have been so thoughtful and ask her if she would like to have a cup of tea. She says she will take a rain check on it and invites me over to her place. She then peeps into the bedroom and gazes at Rohit who is fast asleep. Rohit does look angelic with his black curls framing his rather large forehead and that smooth, soft baby skin.

A huge smile stretches over Mrs Billimoria's face and she says, 'God bless, my dear. Those who have children are indeed blessed.'

Her statement really makes me feel good, something that I haven't felt in a long time.

'I agree,' I say softly, as I see her off to the door.

'And oh, before I forget,' she says, 'There is a bunch of letters that have arrived over a couple of years. I have held on to them, meaning to hand them over whenever I see someone in this flat. Are you the owner or the tenant here?' she asks.

'I am the owner, and I'll collect them when I give you back the custard bowl. Thanks so much,' I say.

She waves an acknowledgement and then she is off.

I cautiously taste the custard as soon she is gone. It is delicious! I am certain that Tanya will love this little treat when she comes back from school. I am happy that she has not pried at all about why I am here. Maybe all old ladies are not really nosy as I had first assumed. I am suddenly thankful for Mrs Billimoria's interference in our daily routine.

But regular routines can only so much as take a ripple or two in them, especially now that I am a single parent. My immediate problem is that of cash. I definitely do not want to call Samir and take his handout money for my monthly expense. I am too proud and too independent for that.

I remember the bank account that I maintained when

I used to work at Point to Point. I had not operated it ever since I got married, which means that money has not been touched for eight years now. Somehow as soon as I got married, Tanya soon arrived, and after that too there was no real need for me to use it, as Samir had given me the add-on card. Now I want to revive that account and I want to know how much money there is.

I make a call to the bank and am told that the account has turned dormant. When I ask what it means, the guy at the other end says 'Ma'am, once an account turns inactive or dormant, you can't perform several operations.'

He explains that that in case of an inactive account, you cannot request that a cheque book be issued. After two years of being inactive, the account turns dormant. You can't request that the address be changed, the signature be modified, a joint holder be added or deleted, or an ATM or debit card be renewed. You will also not be able to withdraw money from an ATM or carry out any transaction through internet banking or a branch of the bank. However, the interest gets accrued and continues to get credited over time.

I ask him what I should do to make the account active again and he says that I will have to go to the bank and fill up a formal application, giving a letter stating the reason for absence and also supplying a proof of identity.

I tell him that I will be there in half an hour and set out, carrying baby Rohit. The distance is too short to take a cab but too long to walk with baby Rohit in my arms. But I have no choice and two hours later, all the formalities are done. My ATM card would be given to me after two days and I am really happy because I never expected so much money to be there in my account. I have about two lakh rupees and one thousand in cash, with the interest included. I am glad that I saved up on almost all my earnings, except for the rare shopping binges for clothes, before I married Samir. Two lakhs is a tidy sum indeed, and my immediate problem of getting cash for daily expenses without having to ask Samir is temporarily solved. I don't even know how much money I would need in a month to run a house because I have never had to really bother about money since my marriage. I realize now how much I had *really changed* when I married Samir. It was as though I had handed over the financial reins to him while simply taking a backseat. I had been content to do so.

I was too blind then, too euphoric, and too caught up in that magic world of newlyweds, where nothing matters but the two of them. Samir too had never mentioned the word money, as he had always wanted me to have the best of everything.

'Nisha, I want you to have all that your heart desires, because you deserve it,' he had said, as he had given me the add-on credit card.

My ATM card arrives in two days as promised, and even though for thousands of people who have bank accounts, it is a routine matter where they don't even think twice, it is a big moment for me. I finally have my own money. I treat it with reverence and carefully put it away in my purse. At that moment, that is my dearest possession, apart from my children.

The children and I have settled into our new lives now. Tanya had of course demanded an explanation as to why we were here.

'Baby, sometimes two grown-up people have a fight. Then they live separately. Your papa and I have had a fight,' I say.

'So we will not go back to the big house?' she asks innocently.

'No, this is our home for now. Do you like it? I lived here as a little girl. Your mama has grown up in this house.'

'It is nice, Mummy, but the other house is really nicer,' she says with piercing honesty that only children are capable of.

'I know, baby. We will do up this house also nicely, okay?'

'Okay, Mummy. But I have to ask you something. Why didn't you say sorry to Papa?' she asks with hands on her hips.

'I tried baby, I tried my best, but he would not listen,' I say.

'Don't worry, Mummy. I know Papa will come after some time and pick us up and say sorry to you,' she says with certainty.

There is a lump in my throat, as I turn and blink away the tears.

Samir's call comes after about twenty days of settling into our new home, shattering the serenity and calmness of the routine that I had woven around the children and me. It is like a huge boulder that has been thrown into a placid lake.

My palms go cold when I see his name flashing on my screen. My heartbeats increase. A thin film of sweat appears on my forehead. I had tried so much to talk to him earlier and he had repeatedly ignored. I am too hurt and upset. Why should I talk to him now?

I ignore his call and continue with my cooking. He calls again. And then, again.

This time I pick up the call, and before he has a chance to say anything, I say 'Fuck off, bastard, and leave me and my children alone.' Then I hang up and switch off the mobile, my hands trembling as I do so.

I feel a supreme sense of satisfaction in having done this. I do know that the money I have will not sustain me forever, but I also know that I do not want even a penny from him from now on.

I am determined to raise my children with my money. He can truly fuck off from my life and be with his Maya or whoever his floozy is.

I make myself a cup of tea and call up Chetana.

'Hey babe! How nice that you called! How are you? How are Tanya and Rohit?' she askes chirpily.

'Not so good yaar, I have moved out. Samir has left me,' I say, and my words feel like pellets of lead rolling off my tongue.

There is a stunned silence at the other end as she tries to make sense of what I have just told her.

'You are not joking or playing the fool, are you?' she asks finally in a small voice, hoping that I would tell her it is a joke.

'I am in my dad's house. It's been nearly three weeks since I moved here. Well, actually it is my house now,' I say, forcing a little laugh.

'Nisha, I am truly shell-shocked. I want to come and meet you, but Dhruv will be coming back from school shortly.'

Tanya had met Dhruv many times, and even though he was a year younger, they had got along so well, with Tanya going into the protective 'mummy mode' that little girls so often do, and Dhruv meekly following anything she ordered, happy to be led. Chetana and I had spent many happy hours watching our children play together, as we sipped our iced teas and chatted and relaxed. Chetana too, like me, had quit working as soon as she got married. She was content, just as I had been, being a mother and a homemaker. How happy we had been then. The only difference was she was still content, but my life had changed drastically now.

'Yeah, I know. Don't worry, I am fine really,' I say.

Then I tell her that I have to hang up as I have many things to do by myself now, with no domestic help at my disposal.

She asks why I haven't hired a maid. I do not feel like telling her about my money issues. If I do not hire a maid, my little stash will last that much longer. I don't feel like brandishing my newfound poverty in front of her, especially since I am being pig-headed in not accepting Samir's money. Besides, it is nothing to be proud of. I know that Chetana, being the practical one, will simply advise me to take the money Samir is offering. I do not want to deal with that right now.

Also, partly I am somewhat disappointed that she did not immediately come and see me. Of course I know that she has to be around when Dhruv comes home from school, but she does have her mother-in-law staying with her, she has a full-time live-in maid, and I do know that on a number of occasions in the past, she has left Dhruv behind and gone on overnight trips with her husband. So it is not like Dhruv cannot manage without her. Also, she could have brought Dhruv along and come over, once he came from school. Somehow I feel hurt, because I truly expected her to drop everything and come over, as I would have done the same for her, had our positions been reversed. I don't know if I am being extra sensitive about all this because of what happened between Samir and me, but all I know is that I am tired of feeling alone. I am tired of being brave.

I do not want anyone to offer quick-fix solutions simply because such solutions do not exist. It is my battle and I have to deal with it alone. All I need is someone to just hold my hand and tell me it will all be well. It would have mattered a lot had Chetana just come over. I feel let down.

I sit for a while in my father's armchair, thinking all about it, and then after a long time I decide what to do.

I call up Akash.

November Rain

It is 8.20 p.m. when Akash rings my doorbell, soaking wet from head to toe. The Mumbai rains are notorious, and even though I had assured him that I am indeed okay, he said he was coming over right then. It has taken him six whole hours to get from Fort (where his office is located) to my place. On normal days, it would have taken a mere half an hour, but just a few hours of torrential rains have ensured that Mumbai has come to a screeching halt.

It had started pouring just after Tanya came back from school, and I had immediately called up Akash, assuring him that I was fine and begging him not to set out in the rain. He had told me he wouldn't and had asked me not to worry. I had believed him and forgotten about it then, as Tanya had excitedly started telling me that she had bagged a main part in her school play. She said she had been selected to play the part of 'Puss' in the story *Puss in Boots*. She animatedly explained the whole story to me and I had watched her in rapturous delight, revelling in maternal pride. It is strangely a universal phenomenon that once you become a mother, you feel overjoyed even at the smallest achievement of your offspring. I guess in many ways, I was living my childhood through my daughter. Everything that I was not as a child, she was. She was smart, popular, outgoing, had tons of friends, and eagerly took part in everything at her school. I as a child was socially withdrawn, taunted, bullied, and never made friends. I am so happy for my daughter and I hug her. I tell her that tonight's bedtime story would be *Puss in Boots*, to which she claps in delight and throws her arm around me and tells me, 'Ma, you are the loveliest and best mummy in the whole world.' I live for such moments. I *really* do.

So when Akash had rung the bell, interrupting our *Puss in Boots*, I was totally taken by surprise. For a few seconds, I just stood and stared as though I was seeing an apparition.

'Nisha! You have a visitor!' he says cheerfully.

'Oh my God! Akash! I told you not to come.'

'Mama, who is ringing our doorbell?' calls out Tanya from the bedroom.

'It's Akash, baby. Go to sleep now, you have school tomorrow,' I tell her.

'Hi Akash,' she calls out chirpily from her bed.

'Hi angel,' he responds with affection.

When she had started learning how to speak, I had asked Akash whether he wanted to be called Akash Mamu or Akash Uncle and he had been horrified. 'Please, Nisha! I don't want to be a mamu or chacha or even an uncle! I am five years younger than you!' And he had insisted that Tanya address him by his first name.

'But you haven't finished the story, Mummy,' Tanya tries feebly to postpone her bedtime by a few more minutes. What children have against sleep, I do not know. It is as though she will miss out a part of some great action, drama, which is happening without her.

'Lights are off, baby, and you know the rules when lights are off. Sleep now. I will read it to you again tomorrow,' I say, as I shut the door.

Akash is shivering now from the cold, his teeth are chattering, and he is slowly making a puddle on the floor of my drawing room.

'Good Lord, Akash, I'd have given you a hug, but you are dripping wet. Let me get you a towel,'

'Arre! What is the use of a towel? I need to get out of these clothes.'

'Haan baba, but I don't have any men's clothes. I don't even have a bathrobe.'

'I can sit here in a towel,' he smiles.

'Shut up! You can wear my nightgown if you don't mind,' I say.

'Hahahaha, yeah sure, and I can transform into Akash the drag queen. Muuuuah baybee,' he says in a fake accent and a throaty voice, as he pulls a face and blows a kiss.

I laugh.

'Actually, you can wear my track pants and a tee. The track pants might be short but at least it will be better than the laced nightgown,' I say.

Akash is much taller than me. He is about 5'11' whereas I am 5'4'. So my track pants end just above his ankles. He wears it with my bright pink T-shirt which has two teddy bears and a large red heart in the centre and pretty white flowers all over, even though it is much too short for him. I laugh at the sight of him dressed in my clothes. Then I go over and give him a big hug. More than him, I need the hug.

I am so grateful for his company, so moved that he came all the way in the rain.

'Have you had dinner?' I ask.

'Yeah, I ate a two-course meal while wading knee-deep in Mumbai's streets filled with water,' he says.

'Very funny. Thanks for sending me on a guilt trip.'

'Come on, Nisha. I came because I wanted to come. And yes, I am hungry. Do you have any food?'

'No Akash. I cook just enough for the kids and me. But it's okay; let me rustle up something for you. We can talk in the kitchen,' I say.

'This is quite a nice flat actually,' he says, as he follows me into the kitchen.

'Yeah, if you do not mind the paint peeling off the walls, the floor which is old and worn, and the rickety old furniture, then yeah, it's nice. This is where I grew up,' I say.

I remember the time when Akash and Chetana had first met me after my marriage, and how impressed they had been with the opulent house. Compared to that, this place must be feeling like a real dump to him.

But in a strange way, I am quite proud of it.

There is an awkward silence between us now, as we both do not know what to say about my situation. I don't want to cry in front of Akash. It is still hard for me to talk about it.

Akash senses it and keeps quiet, as he watches me julienne the carrots and slice the garlic and the spring onions.

Ever since the children and I moved here, I have been experimenting with all kinds of cooking. Tanya is as eager as me to try out any new thing I make, and my fridge is always full of fresh vegetables, cilantro, herbs, cheese, and any other ingredient that catch my fancy at the supermarket when I go shopping.

'Wow, you chop like a pro!' he exclaims.

'Wait till you taste it,' I smile as I boil the noodles just right and run them under cold water so that they do not stick. If they are overcooked, they become a sticky, globulous mess.

'So, how has life been post IIM?' I ask. Akash had managed to crack the CAT exam the year I got married. He was delighted when he was placed in Hindustan Unilever (back then it was called Hindustan Lever Limited) on the very first day of his campus recruitment. He had stuck to the same company.

'Yeah, I can't complain. I got my promotion last month. I am now in the middle-management level and guess what I am? A "lister",' he says. He explains that listers are those people who have the potential to become future leaders in the organization and are the chosen ones for a fast-track growth in their career.

I am really happy for him.

'You do deserve it, Akash. I am so proud of you,' I say.

'Far cry from our Parinita days, eh?' he asks, as we both remember our time at Point to Point, eight years ago. It seems almost like another lifetime.

'Yeah, we have come a long way. At least you have progressed from there. You have reached somewhere in life. But look at me. Eight years and I have achieved nothing. It is like I have taken four lefts from the centre and have reached back where I began.'

'You have two angels, Nisha. Don't forget that,' he says, and I love him for saying that.

The doorbell rings, startling both of us. We wonder who it could be in this rain. It is Mrs Billimoria from next door, and this time she has brought along the most divine-looking chocolate mousse.

'Thought you might enjoy this, dear, but keep it in the fridge. I also got you the letters that I had been holding onto,' she says, walking in to place the mousse as well as the bunch of letters on the table, when she suddenly spots Akash and gasps in surprise.

I try hard to suppress my giggles, as he does look ridiculous sitting there, solemnly dressed in my clothes.

'Mrs Billimoria, this is Akash, a good friend of mine. He is wearing my clothes because he got drenched in the rain,' I find myself explaining.

'Oh, hello,' she says, and she hurries out without another word.

Akash and I collapse in laughter like two little children who have stolen cookies and got away with it.

Finally, when the laughing fit subsides, I say, 'Let me go check on my cooking. It must be done.'

'It smells heavenly, Nisha,' says Akash and he is right. It does smell heavenly.

I set the table properly. It is a long time since I have done that. If it is just Tanya and me, we sometimes don't even bother to come to the dining table. We sit with food in our plates on the sofa and eat. It feels good to set the table properly and I take out the old crockery owned by my parents.

The end result is a really alluring and inviting meal and I watch quietly as Akash tucks into it.

'Mmmm Nisha, you're a goddess in the kitchen... too good,' he gushes between mouthfuls.

I feel so happy with his compliments, and am beaming with delight.

After he finishes, he helps me clear up the table.

'Goodness, Nisha, you have cooked a lot. There is so much food left,' he says.

'I am so used to cooking for large numbers when I am entertaining, that I really find it hard to just cook for one. Never mind, let's put it in the fridge so that I don't have to cook tomorrow. Besides, it's been a long time since I cooked Chinese food for Tanya.'

Then I serve the chocolate mousse that Mrs Billimoria has brought and ask Akash if he wants to eat it in the balcony. It's still raining, but the balcony is shielded well.

We carry our chocolate mousse and sit in silence. It is that kind of quietness which is comforting, but only if two people have known each other for a very long time and are happy in each other's company. The rain is a slight drizzle now, and we watch the city lights shining and reflecting in the water, punctuated by one or two scooters and cabs slowly trying to limp back to life. Rains have a way of adding beauty to even the most common of scenes, transforming them into something almost magical.

We sit in absolute silence long after we have finished the mousse and finally Akash says that he should be getting back.

'Don't be silly! You stay here tonight. Do you want to be drenched on the streets for another six hours?' I ask him.

He agrees that it would indeed be madness to try and go back to his place just then. So I make the bed in the other room (which used to be my room) and show him to it.

As I am turning to go back to my room, he says, 'Stay, Nisha, let's talk for a while more.'

The way in which he says it tugs at my heart. For a reason I cannot fathom, I sit beside him on the bed.

We talk for very long. Akash says that he was trying to figure out what it was about me that was different, and that I have really lost oodles of weight since the last time he saw me. He also adds that I am looking fantastic. He asks if I have been on a diet. I tell him that it must be all the walking I do these days with Rohit perched on my hips, as well as the housework that I have been occupied with lately. Secretly, I am very pleased that he said it, and I make a mental note to check myself out in the mirror—something that I stopped doing long back.

Akash also completely understands why I don't want to take any money from Samir.

'I would probably have done the same thing if I were in your place,' he says, and my heart goes out to him, the second time that day.

I tell Akash that I want to start earning money now, and that I would not be taking any money from Samir, after what Samir had said in his mail. But even as I say it, I know that I really do not want to take up a job, as I would hate to leave Rohit in a crèche, and I want to be there when Tanya comes back from school. I also remind Akash about the nightmare I faced eight years ago, when I had gone for a round of interviews after losing my job at Point to Point. I am so much older now, and I do not think I can really subject myself to interviews like that anymore.

Akash is quiet for a while as he listens patiently, absorbing every little detail that I tell him.

'So basically, what you are saying is that if you can have a job where you can be around when Tanya comes from school, and where Rohit can be with you throughout, then you would want that job, am I right?' he surmises.

'Yes, that's exactly what I want, but who would give me such a job?' I ask.

'You yourself would,' says Akash.

'What do you mean? Explain please!'

'Wait and see, but just give me about ten days time,' he says mysteriously.

I wonder what Akash has up his sleeve. I cannot think of any such job and he refuses to divulge details.

Akash and I talk for a long time. He tells me about the string of relationships he had, including two at IIM, after he left Point to Point. He has been through four breakups. I am surprised as Akash has never opened up to me before. Even though we have kept in touch all these eight years, he has not once mentioned any of this, even though we were good friends. I ask him why he hadn't told me all this before and he shrugs. 'Maybe we never got a chance to talk like this,' he says and it is true. I realize it is the first time we are meeting without Samir. Perhaps that is why Akash is more comfortable with being around me now.

Finally when we have talked enough, I say a good night to him as he settles down in my bed—the bed which I have slept in for many years—wearing my clothes. I feel really tender towards him.

And just before walking out, I kiss him on the forehead and turn out the lights.

But even in the darkness, I can feel the warmth of his smile which radiates the joy in his heart, as he says, 'Goodnight Nisha. You know, you're really the best.'

Brand New Start

Mrs Billimoria opens the door to her flat the next morning when I come back from dropping Tanya. Akash has already left. He had said he would have loved to go straight to work from my place, but of course he had to go home for a change of clothes. I had thanked him for coming and he had said there was no need to thank him at all.

'Good morning, my dear,' she calls out affectionately.

'Good morning Mrs Billimoria,' I say smiling.

'You can call me Mrs B. That is what all my students used to call me.'

'Oh, I never knew you were a teacher.' I say. I have developed a liking for Mrs B now. She is sweet and kind and warm. Her students, I am pretty sure, must have loved her too.

'Yes, my dear, I have taught English for thirty-eight years at St. Anne's school.'

'Oh, that *is* really nice. Do your students keep in touch?'

'Yes, some of them do. They still visit me, you know.'

'That is really wonderful, Mrs B. I too have fond regards for some of my teachers.'

'And I must tell you, my dear, I never meant to intrude last night. I apologize. I never knew you had a visitor.'

'Oh no, you weren't intruding at all. Akash is a dear friend and we both loved the chocolate mousse,' I say with a smile.

'I am glad then,' she replies. Rohit gurgles in pleasure, as something in our exchange amuses him, and he lunges towards her.

'What a darling he is! Do you mind if I carry him for some time?'

'Not at all!' I say, as she carries him and he tries to leap towards her flat.

'Oh, do you want to see my house, baby?' She croons to him and asks me whether I mind if she takes him inside.

I do not mind at all and I follow her.

Her home is full of antique furniture. She has done it up so well. There is a huge chest of drawers which dominate the living room, making it look like an altar. There are many black and white photos of a handsome young man. There are also candles and flowers.

'Who is this, Mrs B?' I ask.

'That is my Adil, my husband. The only love of my life. We were together just two years and then God cruelly snatched him away from me. But oh, they were the best two years of my life,' she says, and when she talks about him, it is like somebody has switched on a light bulb inside her. She actually radiates with happiness, her face undergoing a transformation.

I don't know what to say, but I am silent. She is really fortunate to have known love like that.

But then who knows, had he been alive, and had they stayed married longer, perhaps even their marriage would have lost its magic, its charm? I do not know. My own ordeals have eroded my faith in the institution of marriage.

'You know, Adil chose me over my sister. He had come to meet her, but he ended up falling for me. My sister is older. She never forgave me for that. She did not even come for his funeral,' she says.

'I am, sorry, Mrs B.' I say, and I truly am.

'So do you have children, Mrs B?' I ask.

'No, I have nobody of my own now, except for my sister. She lives in Coorg with her husband and her children who are all grown up and well settled now. They keep telling me to live with them, but I really do not want to give up my house here in Mumbai. This is my world. This is where I have lived all my life, and this is where I will die,' she says.

Rohit is slowly learning to stand up with support and he has stood up holding the arm of her sofa. I watch him like a hawk, in case he falls over and hurts his head. Rohit slowly walks, takes his first step without support, and looks at Mrs B and me triumphantly.

We both laugh at his expression and Mrs B claps.

'Well done, Rohit. Now walk to me,' she says.

Rohit realizes the enormity of what he has done and takes a few more faltering steps. He is really growing up fast.

I think for a moment that had Samir not walked out, he would have been the first person I would have called to say that Rohit has started walking on his own.

And some part of me still hurts from not being able to share such simple joys with Samir.

Akash calls two weeks later, saying that he has some really nice news for me, and that he wants to come over in the evening.

'Only if you promise me you will stay over like last time,' I say. I did enjoy his company the last time round; it was a pleasant break in the monotony of my life which is dominated only by my children's activities.

'Yes, Ma'am. But please make the same dishes you made last time,' he says.

'Don't worry about the menu. I will cook something delicious.'

I decide to make some Mughlai chicken, rotis and a lovely salad. I also decide to make a dal. I again lay the table, adding to Tanya's excitement, as she gets to help me set the table and lay out the mats and 'special plates', as she calls them. She wants to know who would be visiting, and I tell her that Akash would be coming over.

'Oh,' she says, disappointment clouding her sunny face.

'Why baby? Don't you like Akash?' I ask.

'I do, but I was thinking maybe Papa is coming over,' she says. She clearly believes that Samir will definitely come.

I do not have the heart to tell her that her papa has called just once in all these days, and her mama hung up on him after telling him to fuck off. I look at her angelic face, and I hate the adults who screw up their relationships so badly after having kids. Children truly do not deserve to go through a broken home for no fault of theirs.

But there is nothing I can do about it.

Akash calls up at around seven to say that he has got caught up in office, as his boss wants him to finish a slide show for his presentation.

'Really sorry, Nisha, I was all set to leave, and the bastard piles this on last moment,' he says.

'Hey, I'll wait. I am not going anywhere. Don't worry.'

And to be honest, his coming later suits me fine, as it means that my children will be fast asleep.

After the children have slept, I find myself glancing at the clock every now and then, as I wait eagerly for Akash. I have brushed my hair and worn a nice top and sprayed on some perfume too. I have never dressed up for Akash before this, but the compliment he paid me last time about my losing weight and about my looks, seems to have worked its magic.

I give him a big tight hug as soon as he rings the bell, and he immediately notices my perfume.

'Nisha, you smell great and you look gorgeous,' he says, and I smile.

'You don't look too bad either,' I say.

'Dry clothes generally look smarter than wet ones,' he smiles and winks.

'Are you hungry? Do you want to eat now?' I ask him.

'Not really hungry. Get me two glasses, I have something for you,' he says.

I fetch two glasses while he opens his laptop bag and takes out a bottle of wine.

'Some lovely red South African wine for us,' he says, as he pours.

'But what are we celebrating?' I ask amused.

'Patience, lady, patience. Let me show you,' he says as he hands over a paper envelope to me.

I open it with great curiosity and I am so surprised.

There is a stack of superbly designed business cards and letterheads.

My jaw almost drops to the floor as I read

The Magic Saucepan
We make food good!

Underneath that, on the bottom right side is *my* name, address, and phone number.

I notice that Akash has used just Nisha and not my full name.

The business cards, look really professional and are so beautifully designed on expensive handmade paper, as are the letterheads. The whole effect spells sheer class.

'Oh my God, Akash, what is all this? What is "The Magic Saucepan"?' I ask him.

‘First tell me whether you like it or not?’ he says, his eyes shining.

‘Yeah, of course I do. It’s a wonderful name and the cards are outstanding. But you still have a lot of explaining to do on your part. I’ll explode if you don’t explain right now!’

‘You Nisha, YOU are in business! The Magic Saucepan is *your* company and we are celebrating your first party order. Woohooo!’ He cannot hide his excitement any longer and he takes hold of both my hands, pulls me to my feet, and spins me around.

‘What? Oh my God! *What*?’ I finally manage to say when he stops spinning me around.

‘What party order, Akash? What is all this? Tell me in detail Akash,’ I demand.

‘Nisha look, you wanted to earn money, right? And you wanted a job where you can be around Rohit and are there when Tanya comes home from school.’

‘Yeah but...’

‘No buts. Listen to me,’ he interrupts. ‘You cook so well, Nisha, and there are a lot of these private parties where there is a real demand for some good food. This is where you step in.’

‘But wouldn’t it be easier for them to order straight off from restaurants?’ I ask.

‘Arre! Haven’t you seen how greasy and oily most of the restaurant stuff is? Besides, they all have the same boring menus. Here you will be customizing the menu and modifying it as per the client’s needs. Quality service, Nisha, will be your forte,’ he explains slowly.

'Oh my God, Akash, I cannot believe this. This is all so sudden, and whose order did you get and how did you manage to get them to agree to it when they haven't even met me or sampled what I cook?'

'C'mon, Nisha! There is something called reliability, goodwill, and trust, Madam! The executive director of my company is having a party at his residence. I know the couple well, and they are both quite fond of me. I had told them that a friend of mine has started a catering service which serves awesome food, and that they would have never tasted anything like this before. In fact, they want Chinese food, and you do cook it so well.'

'And how many people will I have to cook for?'

'Twenty. And you just have to cook one main course and two side dishes. They have roped in starters from a place which specializes in just that. You can manage that number, can't you?'

'I have cooked for about fifteen people once. So twenty should not be that big a problem. But I don't have the cooking vessels, Akash.'

'Don't worry, Nisha, I will help you with everything. Ok, forget all that. Guess what I quoted on your behalf,' he says.

'I have no idea, Akash! How can I guess?'

'Take a guess, a wild one,' he says.

'Err...four thousand five hundred rupees?' I ask doing a quick mental calculation. The ingredients to cook for about twenty people would probably cost me not more than two thousand five hundred rupees, if I am making noodles along with one vegetable and one chicken dish, chicken being the most expensive item amongst them.

'Well, they are paying you eight thousand five hundred, lady!' he says happily.

I am stunned.

'When is the party? ' I ask him.

'It's on Saturday night. We will have to deliver the food by 7.30 p.m. I will come here on Saturday morning and help you do everything. Then I will drive you to their place.'

'All that's fine, but what will we do with the kids, Akash?' I ask.

That was a little detail he had forgotten about.

'Oopsie, I forgot all about Rohit and Tanya in my excitement. I can do one thing: I can deliver the food on your behalf. But wait, somehow that won't look too professional. You will have to come and arrange the food on the table and be cordial with the guests. After all, that is what will differentiate us from the regular hotel delivery guys.'

I have noticed that he has said 'us' and I like it. My mind has already started looking for a solution. Akash's enthusiasm has charged me up. His plan does look very workable. He has taken so much trouble, made those business cards and letterhead, pitched for me, and got me this deal. I surely cannot back out now and let him down. Besides, this is a really good opportunity for me too.

If the kids are taken care of, I really will have no problem going with Akash to deliver the food.

I decide that I will explain my whole situation to Mrs B and ask her if she would keep the kids for me for a couple of hours.

Akash thinks it is an excellent idea.

We clink our glasses finally and sip our wine.

'Here's to The Magic Saucepan,' he says, as he puts and arm around me and gives me a squeeze.

We later eat our dinner, and Akash says it is truly *the* best Mughlai chicken and *the* best salad he has ever tasted.

'And what about the rotis? I ask, greedy for more praise.

'Rotis too. Absolutely the best rotis in the world,' he says in a voice filled with sincerity.

We are both as excited as children on their first visit to Disneyland. I still cannot believe how much effort and thought he has put into all this.

I haven't made any dessert, but have some vanilla ice cream stashed in the refrigerator. I top it with some hot chocolate sauce and we carry it to the balcony.

We sit in silence again, watching the Mumbai traffic crawl along, a sea of humanity, each with their own dreams, their own agendas. Each hurrying to go to their destinations. Finally I say, 'You know what, Akash?'

'What?' he asks.

'You really are the best!'

Then we sit and gaze at the half moon and the clear, star-studded sky, and that night, the stars truly seem to be shining brighter than ever before.

Something's Happening

This time Akash has come prepared to stay over at my place. He has packed both his overnight clothes and his work wear for the next day, as he had decided that it makes sense to leave for his office from my place, rather than going to his place just to change. He is so surprised to see Tanya getting ready all by herself.

'Nisha, you have really made Tanya quite independent. She does not need your help at all?' he asks incredulously.

'Akash, she is seven! She can definitely manage to have a bath and wear clothes on her own.'

'Yeah, but still. You do have your morning routine in clockwork precision. Really, I am in awe,' he says.

'Well, years of single parenting has taught me that to manage kids, the most important thing is routine. I used to handle all their stuff myself. You know, Samir was never there. So everything has to be clockwork, Akash. That is what keeps the wheels turning in perfect precision. But you know, sometimes it gets really boring. That is why a visit from you is a welcome change.'

'Is that the only reason?' he smiles as he asks.

'Plus, of course, the bonus of seeing you dressed up in a pink t-shirt with white flowers on it, and pants, both of which are too short for you, and scaring the living daylights out of unsuspecting old ladies,' I say without missing a beat, and he laughs.

Akash has some time on hand, as he says that he has to be at work only at eleven thirty or even noon. I ask him if he would mind walking Tanya to the bus stop, and he says he of course does not mind at all. He insists on even carrying Rohit in case I need a break from the kids. I find that very sweet of him, but I tell him I will take care of Rohit.

When he comes back, we decide that the first step in putting The Magic Saucepan in action involves taking Mrs B into confidence and telling her all about my life so far. I really do not mind that now because I have started to warm up to her. She is quite an endearing little thing and is always considerate. But I tell Akash that the first step can wait and I will do it after he leaves.

The second step is my speaking on the phone to Mrs Singh who is Akash's director's wife. Akash had told her that I would give her a call. Akash dials her number from his phone, talking to her for a few minutes, after which he hands over the phone to me. Mrs Singh asks about my experience in this field and I tell her that I have cooked for eight years and catered for home parties, which is the truth really. I have indeed cooked so many times these eight years, and have entertained Samir's business associates as well as his friends (whom I truly did not much like, but I always played the role of the good wife) in the parties which we threw. I tell her that Chinese food is my speciality and she will truly have no complaints. I ask her if I can pack a sample for her to taste for her approval, and she says there is no need for that, as she has full confidence in Akash and his choice. The only thing is that she expects me to be punctual on Saturday. I assure her that even though the time given is 7.30 p.m., I would definitely be there at least fifteen minutes early. She is happy.

'You never cease to surprise me, lady. You really spoke like a pro. Well done!' exclaims Akash.

'Oh, being with Samir for so many years, I have dealt a lot with people like Mrs Singh. That has made me understand these so-called "high society" people who think their shit smells better than others',' I say bitterly.

'I assure you Mrs Singh is nothing like that. She is a very down-to-earth person,' says Akash.

'Most of them speak well to you if you have money. I have seen how some of them treat those that are economically less fortunate than them. Anyway, we don't have to argue on her character. Let's get down to business,' I reply.

'I agree,' says Akash. 'So step three, which has to be carried out on Friday, is hiring all the huge vessels that we will need to cook in and arranging for one of those stoves which will hold them. We can connect your gas cylinder to the stove. We will hire the utensils on Friday and return them on Saturday, after we finish cooking. That way, we will only have to pay a day's rent for them. I have already spoken to this guy, Ahmed Bhai, who rents out the stuff. He has assured me there won't be any glitches.'

'I am nervous, Akash. You know I have never done anything like this before.'

'Don't worry, Nisha, I am there with you.'

'So basically, step four too has to be done on Friday. I will have to go and buy all the ingredients that will be required. This local store called Spar stocks some really fresh fruits and veggies which are replenished every morning by eleven, so that should be fine.'

'Hey, Nisha, listen, you will not be able to carry it all back yourself. I will bring my car on Friday evening and will stay over so that get the stuff together.'

'Akash, you're doing so much for me. I really don't know how to thank you.'

'Thank me by making a success out of it. And don't worry, nothing can go wrong,' he assures me.

Then he has his breakfast and leaves for work.

Had Akash even had a little bit of inkling of what was to come, and how terribly wrong things could go, and would go, with The Magic Saucepan's first party order, he would not have assured me with such confidence.

But we are yet to know it then, and I feel placated by his words, and feel truly blessed to have a friend like him.

I decide to execute step one the very same day. When Rohit is asleep, I quickly dash out and ring Mrs B's doorbell and ask her if she can come over to my place for a few minutes, as I need to talk to her. That way, I can be around in case Rohit wakes up from his nap.

'Of course, my dear, we will have some tea and talk. Put the kettle to boil please, will you? Give me five minutes and I will be there,' she says.

I leave the door to my flat open and make two cups of tea, and just as I am carrying it to the dining table, Mrs B enters with a white porcelain plate in her hand, on which is placed a very delicious-looking piece of chocolate cake.

She sees the two cups of tea that I have set on the table and places the cake beside it.

'Here you have it. Tea for two and a piece of cake, plus, of course, conversation. These small moments are what make life worthwhile,' she says, her eyes shining and taking the years she has lived off her.

Her positive attitude towards life and the joy that she finds in small things has me smiling, and soon I am pouring out my whole life story to her, including the situation that I currently find myself in.

Mrs B listens quietly.

'Ah, I always wondered why this flat was locked ever since I moved here,' she says.

'So now you know the whole story,' I say.

'Yes, and don't worry my dear, we have to see The Magic Saucepan succeed at any cost. I will be the, as they say, "behind-the-scenes" support. You already have your executive assistant in your friend,' she says with a glint in her eye. Even though Mrs B is old, she is really young at heart. She is enthusiastic and she uses words like 'behind the scenes' and 'executive assistant', which I think is a rather modern thing to do. I would not expect someone her age to use words like that. I smile.

'Thank you so much, Mrs B. I was hoping I could count on you. You are really so enthusiastic for a person your age. I love your attitude,' I say.

'You can be old at twenty-five and you can be young at sixty-three. It is all in the head, my dear,' she says and chuckles.

The whole week is spent in trepidation, laced with excitement. I tell Tanya all about it and she claps in delight.

'Very nice, Mummy! I am sure everyone will like what you cook,' she says. She is at that precocious age when daughters think that their mothers are perfect and they want to be like them. She adores me and makes me feel so wonderful about myself.

'So, on Saturday, you and Rohit will have to stay with Mrs B till Mummy and Akash come back, okay?' I tell her.

'Don't worry, Mama. I will also help Mrs B look after Rohit,' she offers cutely.

On Friday noon, Akash calls me to tell me that he is stuck again at work and will be very late. He says he really wanted to come to help me carry the stuff home, but it does not look possible. He is upset about it and apologetic too. He says he has spoken to Ahmed Bhai about the vessels and the stove who has assured him that they will be delivered in an hour's time. I assure him that I would be able to handle the shopping and tell him not to bother.

'Anyway, I will come there tonight straight from office, and tomorrow, The Magic Saucepan swings into action,' he says.

The huge vessels and the stove arrive as instructed. But I soon discover that the kitchen is too small to accommodate it all. So I push the dining table to a side, move the dining chairs to the bedroom, and tell them to keep it all in the drawing room which also has the dining table in a corner now. My drawing room now resembles a large kitchen in marriage halls where food is cooked for a hundred people. But this is no time for aesthetics, and I am so glad to see all the equipment that I tip the guy fifty rupees. He thanks me and leaves.

I go shopping for the ingredients and am able to easily get the chicken, the noodle cakes, vegetables, and sauces. But the spring onions and ajinomoto have been sold out for the day. Both are highly essential in Chinese cooking for that extra bit of taste. I speak to the guy at the supermarket who assures me that both the spring onions and the ajinomoto will be there tomorrow by eleven. I tell him I will need a large quantity and request him to keep it aside for me and to give me a call as soon as it comes. I also take his phone number, and give him a missed call to ensure that I indeed have noted his number right. I am so nervous that I make sure of taking care of every possible contingency, as I want to leave nothing to chance.

This is truly a huge opportunity for me and I so want to make good of it.

Akash finally manages to arrive only at eleven thirty in the night.

He looks at the paraphernalia in the drawing room and whistles.

'Impressive,' he says.

'Terrifying,' I respond.

'Don't worry, Nisha, it will all go smoothly, like a knife through hot butter,' he says.

But despite his ready assurances, I sleep an uneasy sleep.

Early next morning, I wake up Akash with a cup of coffee. He rubs the sleep out of his eyes and says, 'Whoa, Nisha, what time is it?'

'It's 7.30 a.m., you lazy bum. Get up now. We have to go and get the spring onions and ajinomoto. I have already started chopping the vegetables.'

'Relax Nisha, we have plenty of time to get it all sorted. And we have to be there only at 7.15 in the evening.'

'Yeah, but I am wearing a saree, and I need at least an hour to get ready after spending the whole day in the kitchen. I don't want to smell like the food I am cooking!'

He laughs, and we both go to the balcony to have our coffee.

Mrs B rings our doorbell just as we are finishing our coffee.

'Do you need help, my dear?' she asks.

This time she looks at Akash and smiles and he wishes her a good morning.

I really would have appreciated help. But the thing is, in Chinese cooking, chopping the ingredients just right plays a major part in the taste of the dish. The carrots have to be sliced just so, longitudinally. If one messes up with the cutting, one messes up with the dish. I had explained all this to Akash and he had understood and confessed that he knew nothing when it came to cooking, and he couldn't cut vegetables even for Indian cooking, let alone for Chinese.

But I don't feel like explaining all this to Mrs B because if she chops the vegetables wrong, my dish would be spoilt. So I tell her it is okay. Mrs B graciously understands and tells me to ring her doorbell if the kids are getting in the way of the preparations.

She is a real sweetheart. I thank her profusely and she waves me away.

Akash says that he can manage to make fried eggs and toast for both of us and I ask him to do just that.

I have washed piles of carrot and have scraped them all. I sit cross-legged on the floor with my cutting-board and begin chopping.

An hour later half of the chopping is done, but Rohit and Tanya have now woken up.

So I ask Akash to fix Tanya her breakfast and I get busy feeding Rohit, after which I give him a hurried bath.

Tanya is excited about all of it. So is Akash. I am just plain nervous.

Finally it is Rohit's naptime, and I make him sleep, so I can resume my cooking in peace.

Tanya sees how tense I am and she does her best to comfort me, saying, 'Don't worry, Mummy, I will watch over Rohit.'

I kiss her and thank her.

Akash asks me what I want help with. To be honest, there is nothing he can do really. He cannot chop, and unless I finish all the chopping, I can't cook. So I tell him to organize lunch for all of us. I tell him to order whatever he wants from a restaurant nearby and he tells me he will take care of it.

I also tell him to connect my gas cylinder to the stove we have hired and fill water in the huge vessel so that we can boil the noodles. Akash does that, as I get busy breaking the noodle cakes into large chunks, and when the water starts heating up, I drop them all in.

Tanya has brought along her book *365 Stories for Children* and asks Akash if he will read it to her. Akash, as usual, willingly complies.

I watch and smile as she happily climbs into his lap, and he begins reading to her about a very naughty monkey who just would not mind his business. I find it amusing to see Akash reading aloud a children's book and smile at the domesticity of this whole scene.

Suddenly, there is a very loud THUD somewhere close by, and it almost makes me drop my knife in fright. It is followed by an ear-shattering wail.

'Oh my God, Rohit,' I scream, as I throw the knife aside, jump up, and rush to the bedroom. The sight I see almost makes me faint.

Straight to Nowhere

Rohit is sprawled on the floor on his stomach, with a porcelain pen stand shattered around him. There is blood gushing out from his arm where shrapnel from the pen stand is still lodged. And there is a gash at the back of his head from where blood is spurting out.

It takes me less than a few seconds to figure out that Rohit must have woken up, crawled on to the table next to the bed, and must have tried to stand up on it, in the process of which he toppled over.

It takes all my will power to control myself from crying out loud.

Akash and Tanya have followed me, and Tanya screams seeing the blood. I am frozen in shock, even though I have picked up Rohit and am trying to calm him.

Akash is right beside me saying, 'Nisha, there is this piece still lodged in his hand.'

'Yes, I know.' I can barely speak.

Rohit is screaming his head off in pain. My eyes fill with tears at the pain he must be going through. But this is no time to be a sissy, and so I tell Akash to hold

Rohit. Akash sits down on the bed and I place the bawling Rohit on his lap. I tell Akash to hold tight and not let go.

I then pull out the piece of crockery wedged in his hand. Rohit leans back and screams with the pain, and Akash's white t-shirt is now full of blood from the back of Rohit's head.

'We need to rush to the hospital. Quickly ring Mrs B's bell so that we can leave Tanya there for the time being,' he says. It is hard to hear what he is saying because Rohit is screaming so loudly. Tanya has placed both her hands over her ears and is looking at me like a frightened rabbit.

'I want to come to the hospital, Mama,' says Tanya. But this is no time to reason with her or make her understand.

'Tanya, no arguments, please? Just do as I tell you. You are staying in Mrs B's house,' I say as I carry Rohit outside while Akash reaches for his car keys.

Mrs B is shocked to see all the blood. She tells us not to worry about Tanya and simply speed to the hospital.

As soon as we arrive at the hospital, we are rushed straight to the emergency room. Akash has driven at a breakneck speed, and now my t–shirt is drenched with blood as well. During the car ride to the hospital, I felt like I was going to vomit. I feel so scared and so darn worried. I am totally freaking out because of the huge gash that is spouting blood continuously.

They have taken Rohit inside and told us to wait outside for a few minutes. I am clutching Akash's hand in sheer terror. My palms are icy cold. I can barely speak.

'The baby needs stitches at the back of his head. Which of you want to hold the baby while we put the stitches?' asks the doctor on duty.

I break into tears.

'It's okay Nisha, I will hold Rohit,' says Akash.

'Don't worry, your son is a tough guy. We will do the stitches first to get the bleeding under control,' says the doctor to Akash as they walk inside.

Both of us are too dazed to tell the doctor that Akash is not the father.

I am all alone now, sitting on the cold steel chairs outside the emergency room. I badly want to call up Samir. After all, Samir does have some responsibility, doesn't he? It is Samir who should be here with me today. Not Akash. Samir should at least know what has happened to his child, his very own flesh and blood.

With trembling hands, I dial Samir's number. It is a number that I have dialled so many times that I can even dial it in my sleep. The phone rings for a few seconds. Finally, he answers.

It is the first time since he walked out on me that I am hearing his voice. It feels like a thousand butterflies have been let loose inside my stomach. It is hard to figure out what I am feeling. It is a mixture of love, hate, confusion, anger—all rolled into one.

'Nisha. Why did you leave that house?' is the first thing he says.

I am thrown so off-track by his question that it takes me a few seconds to even comprehend.

'Samir, you were the one who left, remember?' I finally manage to say.

'You can stay there, you know. I have moved in with Maya,' he says.

I feel like a prisoner whose death verdict is being repeated by the prison warden, even though the judge had declared it long back.

Why is Samir emphasizing it again as though I do not know it? I have no idea.

'Yeah, and I have moved into my own house, Samir. *My own house*. Not yours,' I spit out the words.

I cannot believe that we are fighting over the phone in a hospital while my son is inside, getting his head stitched.

But I am also so hurt at how Samir is behaving. There is no excitement, no eagerness, and not even the tiniest trace of love in his voice. I immediately regret calling him. What the hell was I expecting? A sudden change of heart?

I have half a mind to hang up, but that would just be silly. Also I guess, one small part of me still hopes that Rohit being in the hospital will somehow bring Samir back to me.

'Samir, Rohit is hurt,' I say.

'Oh,' he says.

And then there is silence.

I hate him at that moment. I hate him with all my heart. What kind of a man *is* he? Has his heart turned to stone? Has Maya blinded him so much that he cannot see just how much the mother of his children needs him at this moment?

Finally he says, 'How did he get hurt?'

'I am calling from the hospital Samir. How he got hurt is not important. He is inside the emergency room now. Anyway, I am sorry I bothered you in the first place,' I say and I hang up.

I wait desperately for the phone to ring. I want Samir to call back and ask which hospital I am at and whether Rohit is going to be okay. I want some shred of evidence that he does care for us. I want him to tell me to come home. I want to know whether his children matter to him at all. How can he wash his hands off us this much?

His call never comes.

I die a thousand deaths, waiting outside the emergency room. I sit with my face buried in my palms, trying to remember all the prayers I know. 'Please God, let him be okay. Please God, please God, please God...' I keep repeating the prayers over and over inside my head, in a desperate bid to calm myself. I have never been religious, so I have no idea how to pray. I only have vague memories of my school prayers. I have never had affinity for any one religion in particular. And so I strike up a bargain with God. I promise that if Rohit is okay, I will make an offering of ten coconuts at the Ganesh temple near my home. I promise that I will light fifteen candles at the Holy Angel Divine Child shrine which we passed on the way to the hospital. My stomach churns, and my hands and legs feel like iron bars at the thought of a permanent brain damage or something incurable happening to Rohit. I am so darn tense and frightened. I should have known better than to have left Rohit unmonitored like that. I should have told Akash and Tanya to watch him. I chide myself and kick myself mentally over and over again. I am a second-time mother. I know how dangerous it is to leave a baby unattended, yet I slipped up. I truly feel stupid, and I feel so bad for my son. What kind of a mother am I?

They emerge after what feels like forever. Rohit has stopped bawling and there is a huge bandage around his head.

I break down again on seeing him so calm and I carry him and kiss him over and over. I am relieved to see him safe and also feel awful to see that he now has stitches on his head because of my negligence.

'How many stitches?' I whisper to Akash.

'Six, but we have a brave little soldier here, don't we?' says Akash to Rohit.

Rohit looks at him and gives him a smile. It is hard to believe that it is the same baby who was screaming in pain only a little while earlier.

'So can we go home now? What has the doctor said?' I ask.

'He said that most probably Rohit would be fine, but they cannot be one hundred per cent sure. But since Rohit did not lose consciousness immediately after the fall, it is a good sign. He has also advised us to keep a close watch on him and see if there is any vomiting, dizziness, or an apparent change in his usual behaviour. If we spot any of these signs, we have to bring him back, after which they will do an MRI scan. If not, we're all good.'

I almost collapse with relief when I hear this. He is more or less okay. But still, we can be a hundred per cent sure only after two days. I am thankful that the immediate danger has passed now.

Rohit acts like there is nothing wrong. He is not bothered about the bandage on his head or on his arm. He is his usual active self and is now reaching out for Akash's sunglasses.

Akash chuckles and says, 'That is my boy. My brave baby soldier,' and there is a surge of pride in his voice. I am so grateful for Akash's presence.

I call up Mrs B and tell her that even though Rohit has had to have six stitches, he is fine now.

Tanya immediately wants to talk to me as she has been waiting for my call.

'Mummy, what happened to Rohit? Is he okay? I am scared, Mama.'

'Don't worry, baby. The doctor fixed it.'

'Has he given medicines for Rohit to eat?'

'Yes baby, he has given painkillers.'

'What is that, Mummy?'

'Baby, I will come there and explain everything. You give the phone to Mrs B and be a good girl, okay? Mama and Akash are coming there just now.'

'Okay, Mama. See you soon,' she says, as she hands over the phone to Mrs B.

I tell her that we will soon be on our way home.

It is only when I am getting into the car, and I see my phone ringing and flashing the Spar guy's number, that I even remember about the party order which is still to be completed.

'God, Akash, it's the guy from Spar for the ajinomoto and spring onions,' I say.

'Yeah, so I will drop you and Rohit home first and then go and pick it up,' he says calmly.

'Akash, look at the time!' I say in horror. 'It is 4.10 p.m. and we haven't even finished chopping yet. We have to reach home, start cooking and be there by 7.15 p.m.'

Then I suddenly remember that I had left the noodles boiling on the gas when we had rushed out to the hospital.

'Oh no!' I shout, starling baby Rohit. 'I left the noodles boiling on the gas. We are screwed Akash, we're fucked big time,' I say.

'Shit,' says Akash as he steps on the pedal.

And in that one word, he has totally surmised the situation we are now embroiled in.

We are really neck deep in it. And I don't see any way out.

Trust in Me

As soon as we open the door to our apartment, the stench of burnt food hits us. The stove is still burning brightly, and the noodles in the vessel are an unrecognizable gooey mess at the top, yellowing in white circles in the middle, while its charred remains at the bottom and the sides stare back at us.

Akash and I peer into it and then look at each other. My heart sinks.

The tension of the whole day and this anticlimax is too much for me to bear, and I dissolve into tears. Akash is immediately at my side.

'Calm down, Nisha, calm down. You do one thing. You go make tea,' he says.

I look at him like he has gone crazy.

All the hopes we had, all the dreams we had built up, have *burnt* in front of our eyes and this guy wants *tea*?

'Okay, baba, if you don't want to, I will make it,' he says as he goes into the kitchen. He disconnects the gas cylinder from the hired stove and connects it back to my kitchen.

And he emerges a few minutes later with two perfectly made steaming cups of tea.

'Tea for two,' he announces.

'No piece of cake?' I ask.

'Eh?'

'Mrs B's wisdom. She says it is the piece of cake that makes all the difference while serving tea."

'I am the cake here, Nisha, Want a bite?' he smiles.

'I don't want a bite. I want to chop you to bits. You are the one who got me into this mess in the first place. And look at us now. The Magic Saucepan has shut down even before it started. A fine opening it has turned out to be.'

'It ain't over till the fat lady sings,' he says, and I am surprised that Akash knows that usage.

'I did not know you are an opera kind of a guy Akash. You do surprise me! You know about Richard Wagner's Opera Suite?' I ask, suitably impressed.

'Oh, is that phrase from the Opera?!' he asks.

'How did you know about it if you haven't heard of Richard Wagner?'

'It is a common expression in sports reporting, Nisha. That's where I heard it. Probably at an NBA game,' he says. 'Anyway, why are we sitting here discussing the fat lady's vocals when there is so much work to be done? You go get dressed and wear your saree and everything you had been planning to wear.'

'Yeah, right. And we will go there and entertain them by dancing or what? Ladies and gentlemen, Nisha and Akash will present an item number for us!'

'Arre! Do as you are told for once. Leave it to me. Let me keep our little soldier with me. You go get ready.'

'You are kidding, right?'

'I am not. Now GO,' he says, as he gives me a gentle push and takes baby Rohit from my hand.

The day's excitement has been too much for Rohit, and he soon falls asleep in Akash's arms.

As I get dressed in a very elegant chiffon saree, I notice just how much weight I have lost. I have indeed never been this *slim* before. The saree drapes around me perfectly and accentuates my curves, making me feel so sexy in it. The whole effect is understated elegance, as I slip on my favourite pair of diamond earrings, the ones that Samir had gifted me when we had got married.

'No woman ever hated a man so much as to return his diamonds,' someone once said. I wonder if it is true. But I still do not hate Samir. One part of me is of course furious at his betrayal, but another part of me somehow knows that a part of it is my fault too. The angry e-mail he had sent, did have a huge underlying patina of truth in it. That is why it left me with such a foul taste.

Still I felt we could have worked out things, had he given me a chance. But Maya being in the picture has changed everything irrevocably. It is still a stabbing pain when I think of them together. So I sweep it aside and look at myself in the mirror once more and am really pleased with what I see.

I step out and see that Rohit is fast asleep and Akash has placed him on my bed and is lying next to him. He has smartened up and changed too.

He looks at me and stares. And finally he says, 'Nisha, you look stunning!'

I smile and say a thank you. It has truly been a very long time since a man paid me a compliment, perhaps the last time was before I became a mother! I do feel wonderful.

'Now Akash—man to the rescue, fair damsel. Give me fifteen minutes. You go and leave the little soldier with Mrs B, and then off we go,' he says.

'Can you tell me what is all this about? And it better be good, Akash. I really don't want to leave Rohit in this state with Mrs B,' I say, still not comprehending. Is Akash taking me out somewhere to get my mind off the lousy day it has been? If that be the case, I am going to kick him so bad. The last thing I want to do is go out and eat at some fancy place, leaving my injured child behind.

'Just go and leave Rohit, and don't tell Mrs B about the burnt food and all. Tell Tanya to behave and you meet me downstairs in fifteen minutes, okay?' His instructions are precise and crisp, and something about the way he says it makes me follow him without asking too many questions.

Fifteen minutes later, we are in Akash's car headed towards Fort. I am very curious now. And I beg him to tell me what this is all about.

'Listen to this,' he says, as he fiddles with the controls in the car's music system and turns up the volume.

A song which I have never heard before comes on:

Trust in me in all you do
Have the faith I have in you
Love will see us through
if only you trust in me
Why don't you, you trust me?
Come to me when things go wrong.

'Wow!' I say. Who is the singer?

'Etta James, though Eddie Fisher has sung it too,' he says, singing along.

'Why don't you trust in me in all you do?

Have the faith that I... I have in you

Oh, and love will see us through, if only you trust in me. Yeah...yeah yeah

Why don't you come to me, when things go wrong, cling to me and woh, and I'll be strong

We can get along, we can get along, oh, if only you trust in me,' Akash sings.

I watch Akash humming away the tune, surprised at how melodious his voice is.

It is now 6.10 p.m., and the street lights have already been turned on to illuminate the streets. We have crossed Haji Ali and are now headed towards Breach Candy hospital.

Akash pulls over and stops the car.

He tells me to come out while I am still wondering what the hell he is up to. Then I see a street-food stall, not even a stall, simply one operating out of a cart. There is a guy standing next to it, busy tossing noodles in a huge wok. A delicious aroma wafts towards us, making the food look *very* appetizing.

Then it strikes me!

'No, Akash! We can't possibly do that!' I exclaim, the sheer audacity of the plan poking me like a sharp pinprick.

'Of course we can, and we will. Watch me,' he says.

He talks to the guy and expertly strikes a deal. The guy cannot believe that we want such a large quantity of food at such short notice. He must have thanked his lucky stars, as we seem to want almost his entire stock for the day.

Akash and I watch as the guy pumps up his stove to make a very high flame on it.

'He does seem to know his stuff, Akash. Chinese cooking has to be done on very high flame,' I tell Akash.

'And look at the way he has chopped the veggies too, Madam; it is right upto your exacting standards,' says Akash, as he points to the carrots, french beans, and shredded cabbage, all neatly chopped and stored separately in large containers.

'How can we pass off street food as our cooking? What if they hate it or, worse, what if they discover this?'

'That is a risk we will have to take, Nisha. You need to be cool about this. It's better than cutting a sorry figure with no food, isn't it?'

Forty-five minutes later, we have our main dish and two side dishes with as. As a bonus, the guy has thrown in some delicious fried chicken too for starters.

'Try kijiye, Madam, aapko bahut pasand aayega,' he says confidently.

He is indeed right. I have no doubt it will be truly delicious, but I am still petrified of what we are doing.

Akash has arranged all the food neatly in the serving containers which Ahmed Bhai had sent over, along with the cooking ones, in the back seat of the car. So, this is what Akash had been doing when he sent me to Mrs B's house for fifteen minutes. He had been loading all the containers in the car.

We have ample time now to drive to Malabar Hill, which is where Mrs Singh lives.

We arrive well on time, and my heart is thudding in my ribcage like a muffled loudspeaker.

Akash calls up Mrs Singh and tells her we are outside her apartment. Mrs Singh tells us to come upstairs with the food and says that she will tell the security to let us in.

Her apartment is on the eighth floor, with a huge terrace and a landscaped garden which faces the sea. It is very tastefully done up and even though, in my eight years with Samir, I have seen many opulent south Mumbai homes, Mrs Singh's apartment manages to impress me. The party is taking place on the lawn and the guests are yet to arrive.

She has already placed her serving containers on the table.

The hired help greets us and shows us into the kitchen.

Akash is carrying the main course and the chicken dish and I am carrying the starter and the vegetable dish. We place it all on the kitchen counter and then we turn around and see Mrs Singh approaching us.

'Hello, Akash!' she greets him with warm familiarity.

'Hello. Mrs Singh. May I introduce you to Nisha, the person behind The Magic Saucepan,' he says, as I smile and shake her hand.

'I must say, it smells divine!' says Mrs Singh.

I feel so embarrassed, I want to sink into the floor.

I squirm as I manage a feeble thank you, and Akash shoots me a warning look.

Mrs Singh says that she wants to serve it in *her* serving bowls as they coordinate with the plates, while the refills can be had from the kitchen.

She opens the containers we placed on the kitchen counter, inspects them, and says that it does smell delicious. And then she asks about the starter and says that she had not ordered it.

'Oh that is complimentary, Mrs Singh. It is a kind of fried chicken which will go perfectly well with the drinks you serve. I do hope you like it,' I manage to say.

Her face breaks into a smile, and she assures me that she will surely taste it later.

I ask Mrs Singh if I can arrange the food on the table, and also ask her if she wants me to stay around for the full duration of the party. I expect her to say a yes, but she surprises me when she tells me that she has enough staff who can handle the serving and the refills. She says it is the food that she was very particular about, and since Akash had raved so much about me, she wanted to try it.

I thank her politely, but inside I am terrified she will find out about our little deception. This is how conmen and people who commit frauds must feel after duping innocent people. I find it very hard to hold on to the truth, and it is only Akash's soul-piercing warning looks that stop me.

I ask Mrs Singh if there is anything else she needs or

whether we can leave. She asks me to wait and then brings her cheque book. She asks whose name the cheque should be made in favour of, and I tell her my maiden name, while I watch her writing out a cheque for eight thousand five hundred rupees.

I thank her once again for the opportunity to serve her and tell her I hope she likes the food.

Akash and I walk towards the car and, once inside, he suddenly leans over and gives me a kiss on the cheek, saying, 'You were terrific lady. Simply terrific!'

I squeeze his hand tightly and say nothing.

In the car, Akash says, 'Nisha, it's been such a long day. Let us have a drink before we get home. I know just the place and they have tables facing the ocean too.'

I badly want to. But when you become a parent, you sign off forever your rights to live a life for yourself. Every little decision, even the seemingly inconsequential ones like which restaurant to eat food in, have to be carefully thought of and weighed to see if they have high chairs, and whether they hand out printouts and crayons for colouring, all so that your kids can amuse themselves and hopefully let you eat in peace.

I tell Akash that we have to hurry back home as Tanya has been at Mrs B's house for almost a whole day now. Plus, we also need to keep a close watch on Rohit's condition as per the doctor's instructions.

'Right. How silly that I even suggested it. Sorry, Nisha! I can be such an idiot sometimes,' says Akash.

I look at him in the semi-darkness, driving that car, his face lit by the street lights. He is twenty-seven and he is not even a husband, let alone a father. Yet, the maturity he has displayed today, the fact that he has been around with me all through, and the fact that he is now apologizing so contritely, fills me up with an indescribable tenderness towards him. He could be in a pub right now, with young women his age, getting drunk, dancing and enjoying life. Instead, he chooses to spend his weekend in a hospital with *me,* a woman with two children.

I lean over and give him a kiss and his face breaks into a big smile.

'You are not an idiot, Akash. You just aren't a parent yet.' I say softly.

But he doesn't seem to have heard much as he shouts 'woohooo' and turns up the volume on the stereo on our way towards my home.

My Friend of Misery

Once home, we ring the bell to Mrs B's apartment. It looks as though we have woken her up from deep slumber as she takes a long time to open. As she slowly opens the door, she looks as though she will drop off to sleep any moment, and I do feel bad for her. Even at my age, looking after two children is no easy job. So for her, it must have been really hard to keep a watch on Rohit.

'Hello, how did it go? Both the children are fast asleep,' she says in a low voice.

'Really sorry if I woke you up Mrs B, but we got here as fast as we could,' I say in a whisper.

'That's okay, I was reading and waiting for you,' she says.

Akash says that he will carry Tanya while I can carry Rohit.

Ten minutes later, both children are tucked safely into bed.

'Let's do one thing Nisha, let us shift this table and push the bed against the wall. That way, Rohit will have less chances of trying to climb out.' he says.

That makes sense. So we move the table and push the bed to the wall, with the two sleeping children on it.

Then I make a barrier at the foot of the bed with two pillows. I also pull out an old mattress so that in case Rohit falls again, he would be cushioned by the mattress.

Akash and I go and sit in the drawing room.

Akash looks at me again and says, 'God, Nisha, you really *are* beautiful.'

I have the grace to blush.

Even at my age.

Even though I am older.

And even though I am a mother of two children.

And I am surprised. It's been ages since I felt this way.

And with that one statement, and with that look in his eyes, we both know he has crossed that fine line which separates friendship from a deeper relationship between a man and a woman. He has altered forever what existed as a pure friendship between us, and there is no going back now.

I do not know how to handle it, and so I try to cover up. 'Let us celebrate, Akash. Let's pour ourselves a drink. To the first successful order execution of The Magic Saucepan,' I say.

Akash gets two glasses and pours out the remaining wine from the day he had come over with it. We are sitting right next to each other, amidst the hired vessels, the burnt noodles, and other stuff spread around in the drawing room. We are sitting right next to each other on the sofa, and I slowly prop up my feet on the centre table. Akash puts his arm around me and slowly places his left foot over mine, taking my right arm in his left.

The air around us is thick with the sexual tension between us.

Of course I know where all this is leading to. The only man I have ever had sex with is Samir. And somehow, after I became a mother, I had stopped feeling desirable. I am always Tanya's mum or Rohit's mum. But, tonight I feel different. Akash looks at me with passion, and to think that I am driving him crazy with desire is *hugely* flattering. I have a sudden desire to give in, to surrender myself completely to him. Plus, there is a subconscious desire to get back at Samir, no matter how much I refuse to confront it on the surface.

The top portion of my saree has ridden across my blouse and my breasts beckon invitingly. I make no attempt to push it back and cover myself. I can hear Akash's breath quickening. I turn towards him and pull his face towards mine and we kiss. It is a kiss of hunger, a kiss of desire and longing, a kiss which expresses just how deeply he feels for me.

I find desire coursing through my veins. I don't even remember the last time I had sex with Samir; perhaps it was before Rohit was born. And then too, it was just sex with Samir. *Married sex* which has a pattern of familiarity and comfort. It is all good in the beginning, but after two or three years, it becomes boring. Even foreplay usually degenerates to just a nudge and a poke. Of course, the arrival of children does have a way of putting a full stop on the libido. Children are natural, walking, talking contraceptives.

But tonight, in my blue chiffon saree, sitting next to Akash with our arms and legs wrapped around each other and our mouths exploring each other, I forget to be a mother. I have been one for far too long. Tonight, I finally remember that I am a woman too. I want him inside me more than anything else at that moment. I reach out for his shirt and find the gap between the buttons, hungrily slipping my hand in.

But he takes my hand and kisses it.

And then he stops me. 'No Nisha. Let's not do this,' he says.

I am surprised.

'Nisha, I want you more than anything else in the world, but no, let us not have sex. Let us wait.'

I wonder what has come over him. One minute he is kissing me so darn passionately and setting my body on fire, and the other moment he is pouring water all over it.

He kisses me gently on my mouth again and says in almost a whisper, 'With all my other girlfriends put together, they never made me feel quite this way. It was just sex, even though I had fooled myself into believing I loved them. I never had. It was you that I was looking for in them, Nisha. It was you all along.'

'So now you have me, Akash.'

'But what we have, I don't want it to be about sex alone. It is something far more powerful. Let us preserve its sanctity. You have had two glasses of wine. I want you to be sure, Nisha. I want you to be dead certain about what you are doing. Don't get me wrong, Nisha. I love you and respect you. I always will. I always had. Even before you married Samir.'

The enormity of what he has said sinks in slowly like a drifting leaf falling down in autumn winds.

'Oh my God. Why didn't you tell me all those years back then, Akash?' I ask.

'What life could I have given you back then? I was just a graduate then and I was only twenty-one, Nisha! I did not even have my IIM degree, and Point to Point was just a stopgap arrangement till I figured out what I wanted to do with my life. And by the time I realized it, you were already married and expecting too.'

'Yeah, I was in a big hurry to marry Mr Right and become a mother, wasn't I? And I got what I wanted, and now it is a fine price I have paid.'

'All I can say is that Samir is a fool. Can't he see that he has a beautiful wife who loves him deeply and who has given him two little angels?' I contemplate on what he has said. He is partly right, but he is wrong too.

'In the end, what it amounts to is that I just wasn't good enough, Akash. I agree I did make mistakes, but still I do feel it did not call for such a drastic step. Then again, maybe I have been a good mother, but I don't think I had ever been a good wife, Akash. I am to blame too.'

'Just stop thinking about all this. What has happened has happened. We can analyse it a million times and still it will not change anything.'

He kisses me once again and gently escorts me to the bed. I am too drowsy now to even bother to change out of the saree. The day's events have finally caught up with me and I can barely stay awake now. I slowly sink into blissful sleep. And the last thing I remember is Akash covering me with a blanket and tucking me in.

The next day is a Sunday, and Akash wakes me up with tea and buttered toast arranged neatly in a wooden tray.

'Wow! You are up early, and who told you to make all this?' I ask him.

'At least say thanks,' he says in mock anger.

'Thank you, Akash. That's really sweet of you,' I say and he smiles.

'I had to wake up early. Those guys will be here in ten minutes to take away all these vessels. We will have to pay a little extra because we burnt one vessel.'

'Never mind. I wonder what Mrs Singh thought of the food, though.'

He smiles a broader smile and shows me a text which reads:

'Thank you Akash for recommending The Magic Saucepan. The food was appreciated by everybody and the party was a grand success. I have texted your friend too. Mrs Singh

'Wow! ' I exclaim, as I reach for my mobile and read her text. She has thanked me for the wonderful food and has said that the party was a huge hit.

One part of me is hugely relieved, but the other part is also appalled at how causally and easily we have pulled off this deception. We decide to bury our little secret there and then.

Two days later, after Tanya leaves for school, I get a call from an unknown number asking if it is The Magic Saucepan. When I respond in the affirmative, the lady at the other end says she was a guest at Mrs Singh's party and that she had really enjoyed the food. She says that she had taken my number from Mrs Singh. She wants to know if I can cook Indian food for eight people for a party to be held this Saturday. She says she can get the food picked up if I tell her the time. She wants two curries and a dry-chicken dish. She says she has a house help who makes good rotis and will also be making jeera rice, and she needs only the curries and the chicken. I tell her it will not be a problem.

As soon as she hangs up, I call up Akash and convey the news to him in excitement.

'You will get more orders, Nisha. Just you wait and watch,' he says and he is so certain.

He wants to know if he can come over on Saturday to help me.

I tell him that he can come over and look after the kids. I also decide that I would be frying all the masalas one night before itself so that nothing goes amiss this time a round.

Chetana calls the next day and asks if I will be home as she wants to come over with Dhruv.

While I am a bit hurt that she did not come when I had called her some days ago , I am also happy that she has now made the effort to call and wants to come and see me. I tell her to come over.

When Tanya comes back from school, I tell her that Dhruv will be coming to play and she is very excited.

She keeps asking how much more time is left for them to ring our doorbell. She asks so many times that I wish I had not told her that they were coming.

Finally, they arrive.

The first thing Chetana says upon seeing me is, 'Oh my God, Nisha, you have lost so much weight! Are you ill or something?'

I do not know if she means it as a jibe. I just take that as a left-handed compliment and decide to ignore it.

'Come in and sit down,' I tell her.

She comes in and looks around incredulously. 'Oh! This is your *real* house? It's really tiny compared to your other one, right?' she says sweetly, still smiling.

I want to tell her to wipe that smirk off her face. I thought she was my *friend*. I thought that she had come to genuinely see me and to offer some kind of support But it is very evident that she has come simply to feel good about herself.

She has come to gloat over how much I have 'fallen'. She has come to judge my living style and my home.

And I feel like a naive fool to have called her up in the first place. I want to tell her all this. I want to tell her to stop acting like her comments are very innocent and that she is a true friend. I want to tell her that her comments hurt like hell.

But I continue sitting there, smiling a big, stupid smile, pretending everything is okay.

Lean on Me

Sometimes, even the so-called 'closest' friends say and do things that hurt a lot. But when we have been friends for so long, one just chooses to brush these aside as small things and continue. That is a mistake most of us make, and that is indeed a mistake that I made when Chetana came over that day. It was a mistake that cost me a friendship. Had I spoken up and told her how I had *really* felt, maybe my friendship with her could have been saved.

Then again, perhaps everything in life comes with an expiry date. Whatever it was, I learnt a good lesson that day about how situations that we face in our lives change us as people, and how it forever alters the way we relate to others, especially with our closest friends.

I was at a most vulnerable stage in my life. All I wanted from Chetana were a few kind words of encouragement as a good friend. After Samir left me, I was full of doubts about myself. I was struggling to manage on my own, with only Akash as a big backup. But Chetana brazenly walking in to 'assess my situation' (that is what it seemed like to me) bothers me to no end.

I want to calm down a bit, and so I ask her if she will have tea. She says yes and I walk into the kitchen where she follows me in.

'God, Nisha, it is so hot in here,' she says, fanning herself with her dupatta. 'How do you manage, yaar? This kitchen is really tiny,' she says in a condescending tone.

'It's not like I have a choice, Chetana.'

'You did have a choice. He did not throw you out. You walked out.'

'Look, I couldn't bear staying there really. And honestly, I am okay here. So let us just drop this, okay?'

'Come on, yaar. How can I drop it? Look at you, struggling here. Squeeze his balls for child maintenance. And has he sent you a divorce notice yet?'

'Chetana, I don't know if this will make sense to you, but I truly do not want his money. He had offered to pay me a sum monthly, but I refused to take it.'

'WHAT?! You *refused*? Are you out of your mind?'

'I don't think you will ever understand unless you have been in my shoes. I do not want to be a kept woman anymore, Chetana. I want to earn my own money.'

'Come on! How can you talk like that? You mean to say that all women who stay at home and manage their house while their husbands go to work are 'kept women'? She retorts angrily. I seem to have touched a raw nerve.

'Look, I really do not want to discuss this with you. I am finally doing something which gives me joy. It is something I am good at and I have now started to earn money from it. It is just a humble beginning, but I am getting there,' I say.

I should have kept my big mouth shut about it, but now I had already said it. My words have poured out like a swarm of bees when the hive is disturbed. I had spoken out partly in suppressed anger, and partly because I want to kind of prove to her that I am not moaning and crying because Samir has left me, but I am trying to make my own life and move on. I guess, in a secret way I am also craving for her approval, her appreciation, and I want her to tell me that I am brave.

But she says nothing like that and immediately wants to know all the details about what I have been doing.

So I tell her about Akash coming over often and how he has helped to set up The Magic Saucepan. I tell her about our first order and what a huge success it has been. Of course, I leave out the little secret about how we executed it. That is something which is Akash's and mine alone.

I tell her that I really like Akash and I tell her how he has confessed his love for me, and how he had kept quiet all these years. My eyes shine as I tell her how genuinely grateful I am for his presence in my life. I truly am.

She listens to it all quietly and absorbs it all.

Finally she says, 'You ever seen that movie, *The Graduate*, where the young guy falls for an older, married woman? This sounds like that. Don't trust him. He is just a horny, young guy. And come on, you are a mother to two children. How can you be taken in by him?'

'Shut up, Chetana. It is Akash we are talking about here. Not some average Joe on the street. You know him so well!'

'Well, all men are like that. I find all this "true love" business a bit difficult to digest. Men just want sex. Everything they do is for that. You can never trust a standing penis and you never know when it will stand up,' she says.

Her words singe my very soul. They evoke such a strong reaction in me, surprising me too.

I am both furious and at the same time speechless at her statement. I am so upset that she has taken what exists between Akash and me and twisted it into something which it completely is not, demeaning it to a very base level. Under her harsh scrutiny and the volley of words that she has hurled, the magic that I feel I have with Akash wilts like a water lily left in the sun for too long. She succeeds in making me feel very cheap and slutty.

I want to tell her that Akash had every chance to have sex with me, but he refrained. This was not about sex. There *can* and *does* exist a more powerful connection between a man and a woman. But I know her narrow mind cannot even see or understand what I am trying to say.

Besides, she has already made up her mind about the relationship between Akash and me. She has thrown something that matters such a lot to me on to the floor, and she has so casually trampled on it with her words, grinding it in with her heels. I have no idea why it affects me so much, but it does.

'Look, Chetana, Akash has had many girlfriends, okay? It is not like he is some crazy, sex-starved maniac.'

'I did not say that, but I think sooner or later this will go beyond control. So be careful. And you really think all this Magic Saucepan business is really going to succeed? Just take my advice and go back home and take the money from Samir. Why are you putting yourself and your children through this torture? I am being honest with you and telling you what is good for you.'

I want to tell her to shut up and mind her own business. I want to tell her to stop judging something that she knows nothing about and has never experienced for herself. But somehow I keep quiet and quickly change the topic.

I am so upset with myself for having told her about Akash in the first place. It was something that was a source of great comfort and joy to me, and I expected her to understand and be supportive. Instead, she has only thrown a shroud of negativity over it. What is to be 'careful' about? I do not know what she means. And I don't even want to ask her, neither do I want to know.

Suddenly, I am tired of her visit and want her to go. She leaves about an hour later.

I feel largely relieved, the talk having drained the energy out of me.

I know then that I do not want to talk to Chetana ever again. Our paths are different now. She will never be able to see it from my perspective, because her husband has not left her. What has happened to me is my experience alone. It has changed me in ways I never thought possible. I have faced it with courage. Hell, I am even trying to make something out of my life. She has no right to throw water on my dreams.

I know at that moment that the friendship between her and me is over, even though on the surface I have tried to pretend like everything is fine. It has lived by its expiry date. It feels like something inside me has died. I do feel bad about our ruined friendship and I mourn for it.

Silently, inside my heart.

Akash and Chetana were the *only* two people in the world I called friends. Now I have only Akash.

I am so upset by Chetana's visit and her words that I call Akash. He is at a restaurant, having a meal with somebody from his work, and cannot talk at that moment.

I tell him that something is really bothering me and I need to talk to him.

He says he will call at the first available opportunity. When he calls, I am reading to Tanya, and tell him I will call him back after I put her to bed.

We finally get to speak around ten in the night. I sit on the balcony and gaze at the stars as I speak. I tell him everything about Chetana's visit. I tell him how hurt I feel, repeating all that she had said to me.

He listens patiently and says, 'You know what, Nisha? She is jealous that I have hit on you and am in love with you and not her,' he says.

'What nonsense, Akash! Why should she be jealous of me? She is married and settled. Her husband has not left her. Mine has.'

'Exactly. You have the freedom now that she does not have. You are making something of your life while she is stuck in a rut being a housewife and a mother. You are progressing. She is stagnating. We will make The Magic Saucepan really successful, Nisha. I have full confidence in your talent. Together we can do it,' he says.

His words really comfort me. So much that I kiss him over the phone.

'Aaah, I wish I was there!' he says.

'Come,' I whisper.

'I am really coming over,' he says, and he is at my place in fifteen minutes.

I greet him at the door and lead him to my room. I have changed into a sexy spaghetti top and pyjamas. We make love slowly and passionately. He is so tender towards me. It is very unlike the sex Samir and I used to have. Akash's body is nothing like Samir's. Akash is less muscular and smells so different. Masculine. Strong. I melt in his arms. The way Akash holds me is different too. The way I feel with him is not at all like the way I used to feel with Samir.

And later when we are done, I quietly slip into my own bedroom and lie in my bed, thinking. What strikes me most is that Akash has been so darn considerate that he has taken care to use a condom—something that Samir had never done. And the sex has been fantastic. It was something I never knew because Samir had always scoffed at the idea of a condom and led me to believe that if one used a condom, the sex would somehow be bad. What a crazy notion! And I knew no better, because Samir was the only person I had ever slept with in my life.

One part of me wants to call Samir and gloat to him and tell him, 'I wasn't good enough for you, eh? Look at me now. Ha!'

But of course I do nothing of that sort and continue lying in the dark and smiling to myself.

The second party order that The Magic Saucepan gets goes smoothly, without a glitch. Mrs Brar, who had placed the order, loves the food, and so do her guests. In a country like India, where hospitality and entertaining people is rooted deeply in our genes, there is always a demand for good home-cooked food. And so our fame spreads. We start getting more and more party orders. By the end of the month, we have successfully catered for nine parties of varying sizes at various south Mumbai homes. One is a kitty party, one a birthday, one a 'welcome home' party thrown by a lady for her son who was coming home from Australia, and the others are informal get-togethers. I maintain meticulous accounts of everything. It helps keep track of the profit-and-loss situation. At the end of first month, we have made a tidy profit of eighteen thousand, five hundred and forty-six rupees.

'Wow Akash! I cannot tell you how thrilled I am!' I tell him.

'Told you Nisha, this is just the beginning!' he says.

I am now no longer nervous about cooking for parties. I know I am good, and the word-of-mouth publicity is working wonders for the company.

Slowly, Akash and I fall into a pattern.

Most weekends now, Akash stays over. Tanya looks forward to his coming over on weekends. So does Mrs B. It has become almost a ritual now. Whenever Akash comes, Mrs B bakes a cake which Akash looks forward to as eagerly as Tanya, and I watch amusedly, at the delight on their faces. We all sit together, having our tea and our pieces of cake.

At times like this, I feel so grateful for all these people in my life. Mrs B and Akash are not my blood relatives. But they are my greatest support system, having seen me through thick and thin. If there is one thing that I have realized, it is this that love and friendship do have a power.

It fills me with happiness, it fills me with peace, and I really start looking forward to Akash coming over on weekends.

One weekend Akash brings home something for me. It is a laptop.

'High time you got connected, Nisha. This is for you,' he says.

'Oh my God, Akash, what was the need for all this?' I ask.

'Hey, your company needs it more than you now. Business is expanding and a computer is a must.'

'Then let me pay for it from the company account.'

'I knew you would say that! I know you so well.'

'Don't try to change the topic now. You tell me how much it is.'

'Relax, Nisha, this is not a new piece. Our company is getting new laptops for all the managers at my levels.

So they are selling these old ones at depreciated value to the employees. It costs just twenty-five hundred rupees, can you believe it? And this machine is in really good condition as it has been used for less than two years! And only I have been using it, so I know it.'

I am very happy about it. Akash has got the forms too for the internet connection and within five days, I have connectivity.

Akash says we need a website to help grow the business. He takes the help of his IIM friend—a whiz at creating websites—who loves doing such stuff as a hobby. The friend is happy to oblige, and within fifteen days, we have a really impressive website up and running.

Akash is a real pillar of strength.

By the second month, we have made a profit of close to thirty thousand. With business expanding, we decide to hire a lady who comes and helps with the cooking whenever we have a big order. She is Mrs B's house-help and all too happy to help, me as it means extra money for her too, without her having to take up another full-time job. In the third month, we finally cross the thirty-thousand mark.

It is a big sum for me and Akash insists on a celebration.

Akash says we will not work the following weekend and will instead take a two-day break to Panchgani. He says we would drive there and he knows a lovely place where there is a home stay.

'But, Akash, I have commitments to fulfil for the next two weekends, and I simply can't cancel.'

Akash stares at me for a while.

Then he comes over and kisses me, saying 'Nisha, you are even lovelier as a successful businesswoman. I am so proud of you.'

For the first time in my life, I understand what true love really feels like. And I feel like the luckiest woman on earth to have found it.

Speak Softly Love

Most of my clients are really sweet people who love anything I cook for them. But I do get my share of the usual fussy ones who insist I stick around till the food is heated and served. Somehow I don't like these clients, because not only does it mean additional demands on my time, but the way they talk to me also irks me a little bit. Mrs Singh, my very first client, was a gracious host and a kind human being. But a few of my clients are the nouveau rich, and it is they who I term as 'pesky puskis'. Akash laughs when I first mention it to him on the phone, in one of my many 'crib-about-my-clients' phone calls to him.

'My God, Nisha! Where in the world do you come up with these terms?' he laughs uproariously.

'Hey, what else can I do? I am forced to come up with such names in order to retain my sanity. They create so much fuss that I am forced to make up such names to stay sane. And, listen, mark it in your diary, next Saturday is the Chhabra's party order. They insist that I be there till food is served. So you will be with me, right?'

'Do you need to even ask? Of course, I will, Nisha.'

It is at Mrs Chhabra's party that I see Samir. I had not even for the slightest moment thought he would be one of the guests. I freeze in shock. My heart almost stops beating. He is holding a drink and seems to be in deep conversation with another party guest. There is still time for the party to get started in full swing and many of the guests are yet to arrive, leaving the place looking a bit deserted for a party. Mrs Chhabra insists that I remain there till food is served. I turn around to look at Akash and I know he has seen Samir too. He squeezes my hand to assure me he is with me.

Samir still looks as handsome as he did before our separation. He is busy laughing at something which another guest is saying. It is hard to describe what I feel. This is a guy I lived with, had children with, and also shared a home with. He used to be *mine*. Yet he seems like a complete stranger today. Till now I thought I had been handling this whole break-up scene well, but now, seeing him suddenly like this, all the feelings which I had boxed up and stashed away, come stomping back, making me feel heartbroken again.

It is like an overweight grocery bag which has ripped apart because too much has been stuffed into it, leaving all its contents scattered on the floor. But there is no way I am going to let Samir even see what I feel. I want to be all classy and cool and appear as though I am least bothered by his presence. I know I look marvellous in a brown printed-silk saree which drapes around me so well, especially now that I have lost so much weight. My intention is not to make him feel jealous, but let him know I am capable of looking super, even after he has ditched me for a bimbo.

I can't help glancing at him every now and then and each time I do, it is like a stab going straight to my own heart. Then I see Maya and a fresh wave of pain jabs away inside me. I had thought that I had healed, but this business of suddenly seeing them has only shown me how much I am really broken inside.

And then Samir notices me. He looks in my direction again as if to make sure it is me standing a few inches away from him. I am certain he barely recognized me the first time around. Now a slow flicker of recognition dawns on his face. He is stunned to see me and gawks at my apparent transformation. Even after all that transpired between us, I can still read his expressions like a book. I turn away and talk to Akash on purpose, cracking a silly joke and laughing. I want Samir to see that I am getting on just fine without him. Samir quickly turns away as if he did not see me and I cannot wait to get away from the party.

Finally, the food is served, and Akash and I talk to Mrs Chhabra for a while, after which we leave.

As we are driving back in the car, I tell Akash that I feel lousy.

'Why should you feel lousy, Nisha? It is he who walked away. It is he who does not have the guts or even the courage to face you because he was the one who ran away in the first place, Nisha. You stayed behind in the marriage. You gave it all you got. Too bad it wasn't good enough for him.'

I desperately want to believe Akash. But one part of

me also knows that I am to blame for our failed marriage as well. Samir and I simply did not put in enough effort to make our marriage work. I was too busy being a mother that I had neglected him. There was no fire in our sex life which had become like a chore that one ticks off tiredly at the end of the day like an item on a 'to-do' list. I had indeed changed in many ways after our marriage.

Just as I have changed in so many ways after he left me.

Akash has switched on the music in the car and it is Andy Williams' deep voice which floods the car with the song 'Speak Softly Love' from the motion picture *The Godfather*.

Speak softly, love and hold me warm against your heart
I feel your words, the tender trembling moments start
We're in a world, our very own
Sharing a love that only few have ever known
Wine-coloured days warmed by the sun
Deep velvet nights when we are one...

Both of us listen to the song in rapt silence.

When the song is over, Akash looks at me and then squeezes my hand, saying, 'Never value those who do not value who you are. You owe that much to yourself.'

I squeeze his hand back gratefully. Deep down I am happy to be by his side and he drives on in Mumbai's roads lit up by the city lights.

Akash has to go out of town on work and his flight is due early next morning. So he does not stay over. But he comes upstairs and helps me carry Tanya and Rohit back to my place from Mrs B's apartment. Mrs B has given us a separate key to her house, as that way she does not have to stay awake to wait up for us till the wee hours.

As Akash leaves for his place, he tells me not to think about it and just to put it out of my system altogether. He reminds me that I am now a businesswoman making good progress and that I should not let anybody, anybody at all, get me down. I tell him I will be fine.

Just as I am falling asleep, the phone rings. I expect it to be Akash on the other end and so I answer groggily with my eyes closed, without even looking at the screen to check the caller's name. I sit upright when I hear Samir's voice.

It is like I have got an electric shock.

'Nisha, I need to talk to you.'

I keep quiet. *What does he want now?*

'Hello Nisha—are you there?'

'Yes.'

'Look, I don't know what the heck you think you are doing trying to embarrass me like this by getting into some catering business. Do you realize how bad it makes me look in my circles? I have offered you enough money, haven't I? What the heck is all this nonsense about supplying food to people's parties? And what is Akash doing with you?'

I am outraged at the sheer audacity of what he says. He is calling because it makes *him* look bad? How is it that he did not bother in the least about whether it will make him look bad when he left his wife for another woman? How is it that he did not care about how it will make *me* look, when he deserted ship?

'Just fuck off, Samir,' I say and hang up.

He calls back. I don't even know why I answer.

'Don't talk like that, Nisha. The least we can do is be civil and talk properly to each other like mature adults,' he says, and I know he is fuming.

In a way I am enjoying his anger. I am enjoying seeing him getting all worked up like this. I don't know if I am nurturing a tiny little hope somewhere that we can indeed get back together.

'Look, Samir,' I say, 'I wasn't good enough for you and you left. Now what I do with my life is my business. I don't think you have any right to tell me how I should lead it. You lost that right the day you decided to leave me. I have finally found my calling, and too bad if you think catering is a demeaning job. I do not want your money, your house—nothing.'

He is silent for a long time. Finally he asks, 'What is with Akash? You seeing him?' I can sense the anticipation in his voice. Maybe it's jealousy? I sort of feel good about this, thinking he still cares for me a little bit. His voice has softened and he almost sounds like a little boy asking if he can be taken to the zoo. 'Maybe. Maybe not. What is it to you, Samir? How can you even ask? You are the one in love with Maya and you are asking me about Akash?' I say.

Samir does not know how to respond to that. So he changes tracks quickly.

'Touché. By the way, you seem to have lost a great deal of weight. It suits you.'

'Thank you,' is all I can muster.

Then he asks how the kids are doing. Now that's a rarity. I don't know what to answer. I don't know why he is asking. He was always the outsider, the uninvolved parent. He was never there for any of the parent–teacher meetings, school plays, sports days, nothing. Never once did he take Tanya out all by himself. Tanya of course has grown up believing that this is how fathers are. I want to explain all this to him. But I have no energy. The hurt is too much and there are so many layers of pain, gathered along over the years, piled up one over the other. To peel them all slowly and to rectify what went wrong seems like an impossible task. Also, I am not the same person anymore.

So I tell him that it has been a really long day and I have to hang up.

His phone call has really disturbed me. I wish I had not seen him today. It would have made things so much easier.

But his presence at the party, and now this phone call, has stirred in me a storm of emotions, and I do not even have Akash to hide behind.

When Akash returns to Mumbai, the first thing he does after the landing is call me. Tanya is already in school and I am feeding Rohit his afternoon meal when the phone starts ringing.

'Nisha, I am calling from the airport. You're at home?' he asks.

His voice tells me that something is amiss.

'Yes, Akash. What happened? Is everything okay?' I ask.

'Well, yes and no. I will come there and explain,' he says.

I wonder what has happened. I wonder why Akash sounds so tense. Why has he said yes and no when I asked if all was well? I guess it must be a work-related thing. Maybe the trip did not go well and his boss (whom he never really liked in the first place) must have then said something upsetting.

It takes Akash almost two hours to reach my place from the airport.

When I greet him at the door, I look at his face and instantly know all's not well with him.

'What happened, Akash? Tell me, please,' I say.

'Nisha, they have decided to transfer me to the Pondicherry branch and I have to report there within the next fifteen days. I am being promoted to the post of factory manager. It is an excellent move for my career.'

My heart sinks. Akash is moving out of Mumbai within the next fifteen days. Just when I thought we were headed for something more meaningful in our relationship comes this bolt from the blue.

I feel like screaming at the unfairness of it all. It is like the universe is conspiring to make my life miserable on purpose. Akash has become such an integral part of my life that I cannot imagine staying here alone without his comforting presence.

'Akash, that is really fantastic. Hearty congrats,' I say, trying to conceal my sadness at his sudden decision to leave.

He keeps quiet.

'Akash, I'm really happy for you, but I also can't deny that I am also somewhat upset. What will I do without you, Akash? How will I manage?' I say.

He has no answer.

Neither do I.

To Live is to Die

Akash feels both miserable and elated about this. He truly does not know what to do.

We talk about it every single day. In fact, it is all we talk about. Finally, we accept that there is nothing much we can do about the situation and wait till the date arrives. Two weeks fly. I have four party orders that weekend and two more the next weekend, which is when Akash is leaving for Pondicherry.

He has never been there before, and neither have I. We search the internet for all the information about Pondicherry. The town does not have an airport, so Akash will have to first take a flight to Chennai, from where the town is a three-hour drive by road. The East Coast Road that links the two places together has been voted as one of the most picturesque roads in Asia.

'Wow, Akash, look at these! The sea looks amazing' I exclaim, and then we read about Auroville and the Promenade at Pondicherry, the Ashram which Aurobindo had established. We read about how traces of the town's colonial past are still visible on its streets. After all,

Pondicherry was a French colony for more than one hundred and fifty years. We look at the photos and agree that the place does look appealing, even though it is probably awfully hot.

And when it is time for Akash to leave, I am still cooking for the party orders as he hugs me and tells me he will call every single day. He kisses Tanya and Rohit. Mrs B too has come to bid him a farewell and he gives her a tight hug as well.

Then he leaves for the airport and I am glad that I have something to do which will take my mind off his departure.

Akash calls as soon as his flight lands in Chennai asking where I am. I tell him that I have delivered the party orders and am in the cab on my way home. He tells me that he misses me and asks me to call him as soon as I reach home. I tell him that I will call once I put Tanya and Rohit to bed.

But with Akash gone, it is just not the same. I have to take a hired cab to the places where food has to be delivered. When I come back, I have to carry Tanya and Rohit, one by one, all by myself into my apartment. To say that I am missing Akash would be like saying that someone misses a limb when it is amputated. I feel so incomplete without him. His absence is a huge void. I tell him all this on the phone and he says, 'Oh Nisha, I feel the same way. I miss you like crazy, you have no idea.'

The Magic Saucepan continues to get orders and I continue accepting them. But Akash's absence from it is a real dampener. I miss his coming over on weekends. So do Tanya and Mrs B. Rohit is too small to understand any of this and he, I guess, is the only one who does not miss Akash.

Akash texts at least fifteen times during the day and I wait for his texts. We speak every single night for at least an hour after I have put the children to bed. His sudden absence, and the fact that we cannot see each other immediately, has added to our intense longing for each other. In such conversations, we talk about everything under the sun. I tell him what Rohit did and what happened at Tanya's school. I tell him Rohit has started walking and can mumble a few words now. I also update him on how well the catering service is doing by word of mouth.

Akash tells me about his new job and how he really likes it and what a big challenge it is for him. He is staying at the company guest house for the moment but will move out once he finds a house. He tells me how different the houses in Pondicherry really are. He says they are nothing like he has ever seen before. They are quaint-looking and so very French. He says that Pondicherry is sharply divided into two areas—the white town area which is the nicer part of the town close to the promenade. He describes it and it sounds great. He says the rest of the town is just like any other small south Indian town. He also describes how everything is so very cheap in Pondicherry compared to Mumbai. There is really no comparison. They are two different worlds. After living in Mumbai for so long, Akash finds everything in Pondicherry, especially the food, very inexpensive.

'If I work here for three years, I can easily save up enough money to buy a house here, Nisha.'

'It is already four months now, Akash. Four months since we last saw each other! How much longer will I have to wait to see you? All we do is talk on the phone.'

'When I talk to you, four hours seem like a mere four minutes. Don't you think?' says Akash.

'Yes, truly. It is crazy how we can talk for hours like this,' I respond.

It is over one such phone call that Akash proposes to me.

'Nisha, you know how much I am in love with you, don't you? Will you marry me?' he asks simply.

Even though I expected this to happen at some point in my life, the suddenness of it all takes me by total surprise. Of course, I do love him, but after my previous fiasco with Samir, the thought of marriage makes me sick. For me, Akash is my pillar of strength, someone who will be there for me at all times.

'Akash, you want to get married to me?' I ask.

'Actually, it is Angelina Jolie I wanted to get married to, but Brad wouldn't agree,' he says in a mocking tone and I chuckle.

'Listen, Nisha, I have given some really serious thought to this. My parents are already hinting that they want to see me settled. But I simply cannot go and meet girls and do all that 'arranged marriage' business, when I have pledged my heart to you. It would be unfair to both my folks as well as the girl.'

'Look Akash, I am not even divorced yet. And I do not plan to have any more children. You will, at some point in time, want your own biological kids, won't you? Why are you throwing away your life for some married woman with two kids? And do you think your parents will ever accept this? You are what, six years younger than me?

'Five years and eight months, and it truly does not matter. Be honest, have you ever felt the age difference between us?'

'Not even once.'

'Then? That argument does not hold water. And as regards biological kids, I am fine with not having any of my own. I don't think a guy has to go around sowing his sperms to prove his manhood. You do not become a father by fucking someone and making her pregnant. You become a father by nurturing your child, by being there for them when they need you, by being a role model, by sticking around when the going is tough. Can you deny that I have not done all that for Tanya and Rohit l? I have loved them as much as I would if they were biologically mine.'

I cannot refute that. He has done much more than their biological father has *ever* done for them. I cannot refute that at all. Akash has been there for me as well as for my children, day in and day out.

'That was then, Akash. But things can change. You can meet someone younger, better than me, and then what? You will regret being stuck with me and my two kids.'

'Nisha, you keep forgetting that I have met plenty of younger women than you and have been in four relationships so far. And mind you, FOUR, not one. I think by now I do know what I want. I am not a kid anymore,' he says and gives a dry laugh.

'Look Akash, I really am not ready for marriage or any of that stuff. I don't think I ever will be. I have had a chance at marriage. I have my two angels out of it. That is enough for me. Now all I want is to raise them well and stand on my own two feet. Let us just be the best of friends.'

'Yeah, so who says you cannot do all that if you get married to me? I am never ever going to stop you from doing anything you want and we can still be the best of friends,' he argues.

'And what about your parents, Akash? You are an only child. Do you realize what a big slap on their faces it will be when you announce you want to get married to me, an older woman who is also a mother of two?'

'That is where you are wrong! You know something, my mother had a second marriage. She became a widow within a year of her first marriage and then my father married her. Quite radical for their times, weren't they? Please understand that my parents will really be okay with whatever I choose, Nisha. And here I am giving them two readymade grandchildren too! They should be happy!' he says earnestly.

'Akash, let's just leave it for now, okay? Let's not discuss this,' I say and he agrees to drop it for the time being. But he warns me that he is going to bring this up again and again till I relent. I tell him that if he does any of that, I will stop taking his calls. He laughs, saying I will never be able to do that.

And he is right.

Around eleven on Tuesday morning, after I have bathed Rohit, I see a missed call from an unknown number. I am curious to know who could be calling me at this hour. And so I call back on the number after putting Rohit to sleep. 'Hello, I have a missed call from this number and was wondering who this is,' I say.

By the voice I can tell that it is an elderly lady on the other end.

'Hello, is that Nisha? Sorry to bother you, my dear,' she says. She introduces herself as Mrs B's sister, saying she is calling from Coorg. She says Mrs B talks about me all the time. She says that she has been trying Mrs B's number since last evening but to no response. This is adding to her worries.

I tell her that Mrs B has probably not heard the phone ring as she hasn't switched on her hearing aid, assuring her that I would go and check.

I ring Mrs B's bell about four times. She does not answer. I am beginning to get a little worried now and so I go and fetch the key and let myself in.

As soon as I open the door, I see Mrs B on the floor with a shattered mug of tea next to her. The tea has spilled and seeped into the Persian carpet, staining it. I rush towards her and shake her arm vigorously. But the moment I touch her, I know she is dead. I recognize the stiffness of a dead body, having gone through the same thing once with my father.

My heart starts beating really fast and I begin to sweat. I gather composure and make a call to the ambulance first and then to Mrs B's sister.

Then I call Akash.

He calms me down by saying he will be on the next flight to Mumbai. I tell him it is okay and that Mrs B's sister and family are arriving shortly. Her nephew has already arrived and has taken charge. There is really nothing much for me to do.

Mrs B's death has really shaken me. Tanya comes home from school to see a crowd of relatives and friends next door. The nephew tells me that the body is in the hospital right now and will be taken to the Dakhma or the Tower of Silence the next day, as soon as Mrs B's sister and her family arrives.

This is the first time Tanya is seeing death up close. She is very upset to know that we will not see Mrs B anymore. I hug her and comfort her. She asks me a lot of questions about death and I answer her in a way I know best.

That night, after I put the kids to bed, I sit on the balcony and weep. I weep for Mrs B who had become almost a family member for me in a lonely city. I weep for the frailty of human life. I weep for things that have to come to an end. I weep for relationships that cease to be. I weep for things over which I have no control and can do nothing about. I weep and weep. Loud sobs at first which slowly turn into silent ones. I have never wept this much, even when my father died, and I think that the tears I am shedding now are partly for him, the unshed tears that I had kept inside myself for so long, when he had died. And now suddenly, it feels like a dam has burst open.

I hear my phone ringing and it is Akash. I ignore the call and continue to sit on the balcony and weep. He calls about six times and finally gives up.

Most times when I am feeling sad, I console myself after a while by thinking about my two beautiful children.

But tonight, the tears just don't stop, and I let them flow.

Thorn Within

Mrs B's death has left a gaping hole in my already broken heart. It is an emptiness which I never thought I could feel. Sadness has become a constant companion now. It follows me around like a faithful shadow. Sometimes it is barely noticeable, while at other times, it assumes mammoth proportions to almost engulf me. But undeniably, it is always there.

In some brief moments when I am with my children, reading them a story or playing board games with them, or when I talk to Akash, it vanishes for a while. But later, it always comes back.

Every single day, when I walk to the bus stop to drop Tanya, I see Mrs B's closed door, and the stab of pain never lessens. Many a time, Rohit points towards her door, indicating he wants to go in there. Tanya and I manage to distract him.

With Mrs B gone, my main support system in childcare is gone and business takes a real hit. Some of the clients do not mind getting the food picked up from my place. But the 'pesky puskis' insist I be there till food is served and do not understand when I say that I can no longer come to deliver the food and be on site.

'Can't you send someone? Any reliable person from your staff?' they ask.

I don't have the heart to tell them that the staff, partner, and managing director, are all me.

I feel very alone without Akash and Mrs B.

I could still cope with Akash's absence because whenever it became too much to bear, I would ring Mrs B's doorbell, who would in turn always welcome me with open arms. The world indeed looked better after a chat with her over a cup of simmering hot tea. Now her door is permanently shut, and I feel like a part of me has died with her.

Tanya's birthday is coming up in three weeks. Her school is closed for the end-of-term break.

'Mama, my school is always closed for my birthday. Not fair, Mama! Other kids get to celebrate their birthdays in school with their friends!' she says.

'But you can call your friends home and we can have a birthday party like we always do. Mama will bake a really nice cake for you and we will go shopping for a new dress for you to wear, okay?' I console her, but even to my own ears it does not sound too exciting.

'Oh Mama, I don't want a party this year. I will be eight years old, Mama. I am a big girl. Parties are for babies like Rohit.'

I laugh and hug her; my little daughter has indeed grown up. I sincerely want to do something nice for her birthday, but Tanya insists that she does not want a party.

I truly am racking my brains over her birthday plans.

Chetana, after that day's visit, has called just thrice in four months. I did not pick up her call the first time. The second time, I kept the conversation to a polite minimum and hung up hurriedly, making an excuse saying I had to go. The third time she called, she went on and on about her own life, about the holiday she took in Europe, about how well a cousin she stayed with treated her, and what a wonderful vacation they had. She did not once ask about what was going on in my life, whether I was okay, how The Magic Saucepan was doing, or anything else. After she had rattled off about her own life, she suddenly hung up saying she was getting an international incoming call from her brother in the US.

I really want to do something special for Tanya's birthday now and debate about inviting Chetana over for a small celebration. But the memory of her last visit, the disdainful way she had looked around my flat, and her supremely self-centred behaviour puts me off, and I decide that she being out of my life is a better option.

A few days pass and one day, Akash tells me he is sending me a courier, saying there is a surprise in it for me. I wait eagerly for it. When it arrives, I am touched to see a lovely handmade card by him in which he has splashed yellows and reds and oranges in a thick layer. It looks beautiful. Inside he has written

Our lives have intermingled so much like the colours on the face of this card. They merge, they blend, and they create magic.

I love you Nisha.

You are THE ONE for me. You always will be.

I promise to be there for you always. I will NOT leave.

How much more can I assure you?

I will wait and wait till you say a yes.

All my love and then some more,

Akash

I am so moved by his card that I sit and stare at it. Then I read it a couple of more times and kiss it. I also realize that this is the first real love letter I have ever got in my life. Samir had never done anything like this for me and before Samir, there had been nobody special. I so love Akash and his little ways of making me feel loved. He is such a sweetheart. But if I do marry him, I will take away from him forever, the chance to father his own children. He is just twenty-seven and I am so much older. No matter what he says, I know his parents too will be happier if he married someone his own age.

It is when I try to put the card back in the envelope that I notice there is something else in there too, something that looks like a piece of neatly folded paper. When I open it, I am so stunned. Akash has sent three plane tickets for the children and me to Chennai. He has scribbled a note saying, 'I will be waiting for you at Chennai airport and we will cruise down the ECR together to Pondicherry where we will celebrate Tanya's birthday with aplomb. Waiting EAGERLY'.

I am totally swept away. This guy has style! And he is so thoughtful too.

I call him immediately and he laughs at my surprised reaction.

'I can't wait to see you and the kids, Nisha. It has been so long!' he says.

The truth is I cannot wait to see him too. It has been five whole months since we last met. I am bursting at the seams with excitement.

When Tanya comes from school, I tell her that we are going for a vacation to Pondicherry and we will celebrate her birthday there, perhaps on the beach. She is delighted.

'Wow, Mama! I am so excited. This is better than celebrating birthday at school!' she exclaims, clapping her hands in sheer joy.

She asks me every single day how many days are left to go to Pondicherry. We bring out the suitcases and pack our clothes. The last time I had used them was when I was moving out from Samir's house on that awful night.

'Rohit, say Pooond-eeee-che-reeee' says Tanya to Rohit. She has started teaching him to speak and she repeats each word slowly, breaking down all the syllables for him as he struggles to say them. I smile watching their repeated efforts. Tanya never gets tired of this game and Rohit never gets tired of following her around. He can walk very well now and can run too on his podgy little legs, tumbling one after the other like the wheels of a tricycle.

'Poin-cheee' repeats Rohit, much to our amusement. He is happy to see that we are laughing and he goes around repeating 'Poin-chee, Poin-chee'.

I feel as excited as the children about the trip.

The flight from Mumbai is on time and once we arrive in Chennai, I go the washroom at the airport for a quick touch-up. I want to make sure I look good when I meet Akash. I can barely wait.

Finally, our suitcases arrive, and I push the trolley with Rohit sitting on them, riding along on the trolley and Tanya skipping along happily beside me.

As soon as we come out of the arrival hall, we spot Akash.

'Akaaaaaash,' shouts Tanya as she runs towards him.

He gathers her in his arms and raises her high above the ground as she squeals in delight. He lowers her and plants a kiss on her cheeks saying, 'My little doll has grown up so much! You are such a big girl now.' Tanya revels in all the attention and beams with the compliment and my heart fills with joy seeing how little it takes to make a child happy.

Rohit is now waiting for his turn and Akash carries him as well and gives him the same treatment saying, 'My brave soldier.' Rohit responds enthusiastically saying 'soldeeee' and we all laugh.

Then Akash looks at me. The emotions that we had suppressed for so long, come rushing back and we embrace in a tight hug. It is bliss. It feels so wonderful.

It feels like we belong together and are meant to be.

Akash takes over the trolley from me and wheels it, this time with both kids sitting on it. And then we all walk towards his car.

I cannot help thinking that anybody who sees us from the outside will never guess that Akash is not the father, and will of course presume we are a happy family.

And then it strikes me.

We truly are!

Sometimes, it is those that we accept as our own that become our family. It does not matter if the bond is not sanctioned by law or society and not given a name like 'husband and wife'. I feel more connected with Akash than anyone else right then. And with Akash, it is not just about the sex at all. This is not some young, hot-blooded passion where I am swept off my feet. This is a mature, deeper kind of love. This *is* the real deal.

The drive to his place from Chennai takes about three hours. The East Coast Road is filled with scenes straight out of a picture postcard. The sealine suddenly emerges out of nowhere and the sand on the coastline blending into it looks straight out of an Edouard Manet painting. I roll down the window and smell in the salty sea air and inhale deeply. I love it.

The children have slept off in the back seat and Akash is playing some really nice music. I feel all the tension and worries of Mumbai slipping away. For the first time, the emptiness which had so engulfed me and settled around me like a well-worn cloak in Mumbai, fades out.

'Akash, this is heavenly!' I exclaim.

'Wait till you see my place,' he says, grinning from ear to ear.

About ten kilometres before hitting Pondicherry town, Akash takes a left turn to a small, narrow but well-laid-out road. He swerves inside as the road curves and then drives into the quaintest, large, and the most wonderful-looking mansion I have ever set my eyes upon. The driveway is made of cobbled stones and is lined with tall, gigantic trees on either sides. The branches seem to be bending down and ushering us in. The mansion (it just cannot be called a house) is pale white and has yellow pillars lining a large veranda. It is surrounded by a very well-maintained garden and is full of large green trees. The sunlight criss-crosses the veranda and the shadows make pretty patterns on the terracotta tiles. A hammock tied from one pillar to another beckons invitingly. The garden also has a little fountain and there are ducks swimming in a water body. There are many flowers blooming, and right at the end of the garden is a statue of Buddha. There are birds chirping and the one word which sums up the feeling that washes over me as I slowly get out of the car in a daze is pure serenity.

Akash is delighted at how taken in I am.

The children have now woken up and Rohit is already squealing with delight at the ducks. A guy emerges from inside the house.

'This is Muthu, my man Friday. He looks after the house. He will keep an eye on Rohit and Tanya,' he says.

'Wow Akash, You are truly living a king's life here! This is super-cool!' I cannot hide my joy.

'Come inside, Nisha. I want to show you your room,' he says.

We enter a large drawing room with breathtakingly beautiful architecture. The entire house has high ceilings and wooden roof panels. Even the door knobs are carved and have old wooden bolts running across them horizontally. I have never been inside such a gorgeous-looking house, only reading descriptions of the same in books. It feels marvellous to be inside such an aesthetically done up space.

All the furniture in the house is antique. There is a chest of drawers made of rosewood, there is a large swing in the drawing room, and it also has a small area open to the sky, like an atrium. It is filled with flowering plants and pebbles.

'Akash, never once did you tell me this place is so gorgeous.' I tell him.

'Then the effect would have been lost, Nisha. I wanted it to be a total surprise to you.'

And surprised I am.

I have an entire bedroom to myself. It has a large four-poster bed which is so high that there is a little stool placed beside it just to help me climb into it. The room has deep-blue curtains coordinated with the linen on the bed. There is a lovely window overlooking the garden, right in front of an ancient writing desk. It feels like a peaceful little sanctuary where I can escape to.

'Akash, I have never seen anything so wonderful. Not even in the many hotels that I have stayed in while travelling. This is breathtaking, really!'

'Glad it meets your approval, Madam,' he says with a bow, making me laugh in delight.

There is another room in the attic and Akash says it is Tanya's room. He has taken the trouble to get a wonderfully carved child's bed with amazing-looking carved wooden characters perched on the headboard. There is a delightful owl, a figure which looks like a gnome, a little house, and more. Akash says that there are many antique furniture shops in and around Pondicherry, and when he came across this bed, it was too delightful to pass. Akash says he has already thought of the stories which he can make up about the wooden residents on the headboard, and he plans to tell those stories to Tanya.

Akash has another surprise for Tanya. He takes us to a shed adjacent to the garden and opens it. Inside is the most perfect little bicycle for a girl. It is pink and white and has tassels on the handle.

'Tanya, this is your birthday present,' he says.

'Oh my God. Thank you so much, Akash!' she screams and runs to the bicycle.

Akash says that his *real* birthday gift to her is that he will teach her to ride it. And he does it in two days flat.

I watch with pride as Akash runs around holding Tanya, encouraging her to pedal, and when she finally gets the balance and rides off, he stands there like a proud parent, the sweat dripping from him face with the effort he has put in running beside her. He is truly prouder than a peacock to watch her ride.

The beach is just a short walk from Akash's mansion. And since it is away from the main city, it remains secluded at most times, almost like a private beach at our disposal. We go there every single day, morning and evening, before it gets too hot. The children have never enjoyed themselves this much before. They make sand castles, collect shells, and squeal in delight when the waves touch their feet, watching the crabs scuttle across the sand.

Akash has a cook who also functions as the housekeeper. She is Muthu's wife and between them they keep my children well fed and looked after.

It is the first time since I became a mother that I can totally let go of all my responsibilities and truly relax, knowing that they are in safe hands. It is such a liberating feeling.

Akash tells Tanya that when he was a child, he had a tree house and he would spend hours in it, reading books and sipping lemonade. The idea immensely appeals to Tanya and she asks if it is possible to build a tree house. The large garden has many trees and Akash and Tanya go around scouting for the perfect tree. Finally, he finds one. He gets a local carpenter to come over and explains exactly what he wants. Three days later, the perfect little tree house is ready for Tanya which is also where she ultimately ends up celebrating her birthday.

Tanya is over the moon.

'Akash, this is the BESTEST birthday I have ever had,' she says.

I absolutely love Akash's house, this little world which is so full of happiness and joy. It is totally different from our cramped flat in Mumbai, where when you get out of the building, you are bang in the middle of traffic. This place with its tall trees, a garden, the most beautiful house, and easy access to the beach, is a different world altogether. My life in Mumbai now seems so drab and empty *and* difficult when compared to this. The thought of going back to it kind of fills me with dread.

Tanya says to me, 'Mama, I love this place so much. Can we stay here forever?'

It appears as though Akash feels the same way.

Long after the children have gone to bed, Akash says to me, 'Nisha, you have seen what life is like here. Why do you want to go back to Mumbai? Stay here. We will start The Magic Saucepan here.'

I reach out for his hand and we sit in silence for a long time, like we did back in Mumbai on my balcony. But here, the sound is punctuated only by the sound of a myriad insects and crickets chirping. Suddenly, a firefly emerges out of somewhere, and we watch mesmerized as it flies around.

That night, I ponder over what Akash has suggested. The more I think about it, the more sense it makes.

But I am still certain that I do not want to marry him.

And I do not see how I can get around that.

Nothing Else Matters

The more I think about it, the more I am tempted to take up Akash's suggestion. I discuss it with him the next day, on one of our many walks to the beach.

'Akash, I have been thinking about what you said about starting The Magic Saucepan here. It is not a bad idea, I think.'

'Of course it isn't. When have my ideas ever been bad? Besides, it isn't really doing well there now, is it?'

'Not really. But that is also because I haven't been giving it my all to placate the 'pesky puskis'. I could probably hire a live-in maid there, so that I can leave Rohit when I go to the client's place. But somehow, Akash, you know how unreliable hired help can be. I have heard such horror stories about leaving children with hired help. I just cannot do that.'

'Nisha, move over here. It will be so much easier when we work as a team.'

'I do agree, Akash, but a school for Tanya?'

'I have been asking around. There is a really nice school run by an American lady located not too far from here. We can make an appointment, go there and check it out.'

'And what about the market here for our Magic Saucepan? Are there parties and stuff?'

'Oh, you won't believe how vibrant the night life here is once you get to know the right people. Pondicherry is a very cosmopolitan town, but it will take a while for it to accept you in its fold. I have made a few friends here in these past six months. In fact, I have an idea. Let's throw a party and invite a few people. A select few. I will help you cook. We will put out feelers and see how it goes. What do you say?'

'Yeah, that is not a bad idea. I will enjoy cooking and your place is just perfect to host a lovely party.'

Akash makes a few phone calls and fixes the party for Saturday evening. There are three couples coming and a single guy who is a foreigner. One of the couples sound interesting. The husband works in another HUL factory as the commercial manager, while the wife has a really interesting occupation.

Akash says that her name is Ankita Sharma and that she does art therapy. I am curious to meet her as I have never interacted with anyone from that field before.

We decide to host the party in the garden. Muthu and Lakshmi set up the table beautifully. I have cooked Chinese and all the dishes have turned out well. Muthu and Lakshmi have also thoughtfully kept little stoneware diffusers with a small flame inside that heat up the water with essential oils, keeping mosquitoes and insects at bay. There are several of these diffusers, and the party scene does look beautiful, lit up by the moonlight and the light from the diffusers.

The foreigner Mark arrives first. He is from a small town in the UK called Thetford. He loves India and has been living in Auroville for the past few years. He explains the concept of Auroville and I am fascinated by it. It is a form of community living started by Mirra Alfassa, popularly known as 'The Mother' to locals, and is one of the greatest followers and propagators of Aurobindo's teachings. Auroville is designed as a universal town where men and women of all countries can live in peace and progressive harmony, above all creeds, all politics, and all nationalities. The purpose of Auroville is to realize human unity and he tells me that there are people from seventy-two countries living there at present. There are schools and they have done a lot for the local population. It is a place without politics and it is a dream which is being lived by so many people. He invites me over for a visit. Akash has already been there and confirms that Auroville is indeed worth visiting and promises to take me there sometime.

Ankita is the next to arrive with her husband and two children. She seems very down to earth and friendly. We get along really well, and I am surprised to feel as though I have known her forever, even though I am meeting her for the first time. Ankita's two children go to the same school which Akash had suggested. I ask her for details about the school and it does sound interesting. And when I tell her that I am toying with the idea of moving here, she tells me that as far as the school is concerned, I would never regret it. She passes on the number of the lady who runs the school and asks me to speak to her and go and see it for myself.

The other two couples arrive together. Ravi and Shailu have a large store right in the centre of Pondicherry and both of them run it together, stocking all Auroville products. They have recently relocated from Delhi. They have one child who goes to the same school as Ankita's children. The third couple does not have children. Piyali is a surgeon at JIPMER in Pondicherry and her husband Shibu is a well-known photographer. They all seem like fascinating people.

All the children have formed their own group and are busy in Tanya's tree house, leaving the adults free to talk on their own.

We talk about various cities and about how Pondicherry is as a place and Shailu says, 'I think moving here from polluted Delhi was one of the best moves we made in our life. Here we are raising our children in a safe, happy, and serene environment. The school is fantastic too. What more could we want?'

Akash looks at me and winks as he sips his drink and I smile back.

The party is a great success and everyone praises the food, wanting to know where we ordered it from. Akash tells them proudly that I cooked it without outside help. He tells them about The Magic Saucepan and my plans of exploring the option of relocating to Pondicherry.

'Oh, you can count me as a regular client! This is really awesome!' says Ankita. Mark too says he has a few friends who would love to place orders, as do the other two couples.

'In fact, you should set up a restaurant here, Nisha. It will do really well,' says Ankita.

Long after the guests have left, Ankita's words keep lingering in my mind. I discuss it with Akash who thinks thinks it is a brilliant idea.

We decide to explore the school the very next day itself and make an appointment to see it that evening. The American lady, Mrs Lewis, is very welcoming. She shows us around the whole school and explains its philosophy and the values they stand for. She firmly believes that children should not be taught by the rote learning method of learning by repitition, and believes that children remember best when they learn by doing. She explains the hands-on approach they adopt and the very low student–teacher ratio they have. I am in total sync with the philosophy of the school. It is exactly what I have in mind for my own children. She says they are very picky about the students they take in, simply because it is different from the other schools, and unless the ideology of the parents matches with that of the school, the child will be a misfit. Like everyone else, she has presumed that Akash and I are husband and wife.

The school is indeed perfect.

'So…?' asks Akash as we drive back to his house.

'So….' I repeat and smile.

'Shift here na baba. Look, everything is falling into place perfectly,' he says.

'Akash, right now you are on leave from work. You will join back and things will be different then. Living together is really different from, having me here on a holiday,' I say.

'Hey! How much more should I beg you? I know what it involves, Nisha. Remember, I was practically living in your house in Mumbai? I am not new to all this. And I am not a kid. I do know what I am doing. You are really insulting my intelligence and maturity now. Do what you want,' he says angrily and keeps quiet.

I feel terrible to have made him angry, especially after he has done so much for me. There is nothing keeping me from shifting to Pondicherry except my pig-headedness of being independent. But as much as I love him, I truly do not want to depend on Akash. An idea slowly brews in my mind.

'Sorry baba. Look, after what I have been through, I do not ever want to depend on anyone again. Understand please. And give me a few weeks to think about it,' I say.

'Okay, Nisha. Take your time. I have waited nine years to tell you how I feel about you. A few more weeks or even months will not make much of a difference,' he says resignedly.

Our holiday soon comes to an end and Tanya does not want to go back.

'Mummy, put me in a school here. Please, Mummy. I don't want to go back to Mumbai,' says Tanya.

Akash looks at me as though to say, 'I told you so.'

But I turn away and do not face him.

As I bid goodbye to Akash at the airport, I know that I have to make a decision one way or the other.

Either I can decide that I will continue living in Mumbai and continue running The Magic Saucepan on my own, by hiring a live-in maid or some other alternate arrangement, or I can relocate to Pondicherry and chase a bigger dream.

After the magic of Pondicherry, Mumbai really feels dull and drab in comparison. After having met all those couples there, especially the one which relocated from Delhi, I am very inclined towards moving base. Akash is there ready to give his whole life for me. What really am I holding on to in Mumbai?

Most of the decisions in my life have been made on an impulse. But after my marriage fiasco with Samir, I want to be very sure of what I truly want. It takes me a month to decide. I know what to do.

I call up Akash first and tell him of my decision.

'Oh Nisha, you've made me the happiest man on earth,' he says.

But I explain clearly that I have a few conditions that need to be met before I move there for good. The first is that I do not want to get married and he cannot hound me on that. The second is that I want to buy my own place in Pondicherry. I want to sell my flat in Mumbai and am very sure that it will fetch a decent sum. The housing in Pondicherry is one-fourth the cost of that in Mumbai. Even after I invest in a place in Pondicherry, I will still have a huge sum left with me.

Akash happily agrees to both conditions and says that he has an even better idea. He says we can jointly buy the house he is currently living in. The owner's adult children are all in France and the owners themselves, a very old couple, lead a quiet life in a small town called Cuddalore. They have moved out as the property was too big for them. He says he will speak to them and we can negotiate and strike a deal.

He says that he can come over and help me wind up things in Mumbai. I tell him that we will contact a few brokers and I will move only after I have sold the property here, as it will be easier to coordinate showing the potential buyers the place when I am there.

Once I have decided to move, I have to make another visit to Pondicherry to complete the formalities of admission in the school. Tanya will have a written test, and Mrs Lewis assures me that it is merely an administrative formality. We visit Pondicherry again for a week, and Tanya is most happy to miss her school in Mumbai and go on an unexpected holiday again.

It takes us four more months to sort out all the paperwork and finally sell the property in Mumbai.

As the kids and I bid a farewell to Mumbai city, I cannot help but think that the pieces of my life are finally coming together like a perfect jigsaw puzzle.

Akash is once again there at Chennai airport to greet me. This time, the joy is truly manifold, much more than the last time, because now there is no going back.

Tanya sings at the top of her voice in the car 'We are all going on a summer holiday...'

'And this summer holiday is going to last a lifetime now, Tanya,' I say and smile.

As we drive along the East Coast Road, Akash says to me, 'You know what, Nisha? We really have a unique love story. Maybe someone should write a book on it!'

Epilogue

Akash and Nisha managed to buy the house which Akash was living in, and together they started a restaurant called 'The Soul Garden'. It is doing really well, so much so that Akash is planning to quit his job at HUL and help Nisha full-time. Both have decided not to get married and like to shock people by telling them that they are living in sin. Who says a marriage is needed for a lasting relationship?

Chetana is increasingly discontent in her marriage. Monotony and boredom has set in and she finds no joy in life. Her husband keeps busy with his job, hardly making time for her. But she is staying put in the marriage because she knows no other way out, and is growing bitter each day.

Samir and Maya are planning to get married soon. Samir has filed for divorce by mutual consent, and the court decision should soon come through.

Akash's parents have accepted Nisha and the kids just as warmly as Akash had predicted they would. Nisha is very happy about it. They keep asking Akash when he plans to get married, and that is something that even Akash does not know.

Mrs Kotwal, Mrs B's sister, is in touch with Nisha, and they have invited her for a holiday to Coorg. She plans to visit with Akash and the kids soon.

The couples from the party meet Akash and Nisha often. They always have a great time, and Nisha seems to have finally found so many good friends, something that she had always missed having earlier.

Tanya has settled well in her new school and she absolutely loves the house, as does Nisha. Rohit will soon give his sister company at the same school.

Acknowledgements

When a book is written so many are involved in so many different ways that to name each one would take another book by itself!

My father, K.V. J. Kamath, would have been so proud of me. I truly believe it is he who left me the gift of writing. I owe what I am to him. He lives on inside me. This one is also for you, Daddy.

A big thank you to my readers who write in and send me so much love. You share a part of your life with me and it never fails to amaze me or move me, no matter how many mails I get. You write to say how much I inspire you, without realizing what a big role you play in making me want to keep writing. A sincere and heartfelt thank you from the bottom of my heart.

My two wonderful children—Atul and Purvi—who make endless cups of tea and give endless back massages when their mummy is writing, who are so proud of my work, and who think I am the coolest mother in the world. I love you both, you light up my life. My husband, Satish—who is always there for me, supportive and understanding. He is my pillar of strength and I am truly fortunate to have found him. He was the first reader of this book and was involved at each and every stage.

Mayank Mittal—who read each chapter as soon as it was written. Thank you for making those countless phone calls to me to make me laugh and pep me up when I am sad. And thank you for being there for me always.

K.Ramesh—who patiently read my entire book (even though it was not of his genre specialization at all), and encouraged me a lot. He is a real gentleman and I am grateful for his help.

Shabina, my soul sister, for the countless mails we have exchanged on everything under the sun. I am so lucky to have her as one of my closest friends and she thinks she is lucky to have me.

Rathipriya, one of my closest friends, whom I truly admire and love. She reciprocates, and when we are together, it truly feels like nothing else matters.

Durjoy Datta, for pushing me to work so hard, motivating me, and being so sweet and honest.

Priya Kamath, my mother, for believing in this story when I first narrated it to her and who patiently listens to anything that I explain. It is from her that I inherit my sense of humour.

Suman, who thinks I am brilliant. But I am her 'fooly' and she is mine.

My editor, Milee Ashwarya, who is so responsive and friendly, and also the whole team at Random House.

All my other friends too who think so much of me and who I am in regular touch with, you know who you are!

And lastly, Lostris, who keeps me slim, happy, and content, and showers me with such unconditional love, it is hard not to love her back. She teaches me a new thing every single day. I don't think having fur and four legs disqualifies you from being mentioned in the acknowledgment pages of a book!

Something More

'Music is love in search of a word,' said French novelist and performer Sidonie-Gabrielle Colette.

She sure hit the nail right on the head when she said that.

Since this is a very unusual love story, and since music always adds magic to love, all the chapter names are names of songs.

You might have heard some, you might not have heard others. But hopefully, it might lead you to something you might love. Whenever two or more artists have sung the same song, I have mentioned the version I like.

Grateful acknowledgement to the artists who add magic to our lives with their music:

Waiting for Saturday Night: Dr Feelgood
Luck Be a Lady: Frank Sinatra
Twist of Fate: Olivia Newton-John
All Nightmare Long: Metallica
Some You Win, Some You Lose: Jimmy Ellis
The Unnamed Feeling: Metallica
Happily Unhappy: Toni Braxton
Like a Hurricane: Neil Young
Slave to Love: Bryan Ferry

The Sound of Silence: Simon and Garfunkel
It Must Have Been Love: Roxette
With a Little Help from My Friends: The Beatles
I Can't Make You Love Me: George Michael
Leaving on a Jet Plane: John Denver
Alone in a Crowd: Insense
Every Rose Has Its Thorn: Poison
November Rain: Guns N' Roses
Brand New Start: Paul Weller
Something's Happening: Herman's Hermits
Straight to Nowhere: A band from Sweden with songs like 'Nearly'
Trust in Me: Etta James
My Friend of Misery: Metallica
Lean on Me: Bill Withers
Speak Softly Love: Andy Williams
To Live Is to Die: Metallica
Thorn Within: Metallica
Nothing Else Matters: Metallica

A Note on the Author

Preeti Shenoy is an author and an artist, with two national bestsellers. Her interests are as multifarious and diverse as her several academic degrees, which include an internationally recognized qualification from UK in portraiture. She loves yoga, travelling, nature, creating stuff, photography, blogging, and basketball. She lives in Bangalore, India, with her husband, two children, and a hyperactive Doberman.

To know more, go to preetishenoy.com